THE LUNAR TICKLE

RHYS HUGHES

Published by
Dog Horn Publishing
45 Monk Ings, Birstall, Batley WF17 9HU
United Kingdom
doghornpublishing.com

ISBN-13 978-1-907133-87-9

Cover design by
Emmet Jackson

Typesetting by
Jonathan Penton

UK Distribution: Central Books
99 Wallis Road, London, E9 5LN, United Kingdom
orders@centralbooks.com
Phone:+44 (0) 845 458 9911
Fax: +44 (0) 845 458 9912

Overseas Distribution: Printondemand-worldwide.com
9 Culley Court
Orton Southgate
Peterborough
PE2 6XD
Telephone: 01733 237867
Facsimile: 01733 234309
Email: info@printondemand-worldwide.com

THE LUNAR TICKLE

TALES TO MAKE FULL MOONS GIGGLE

Featuring
Thornton Excelsior,
his friends, enemies and avatars,
with the author and reader
in cameo roles

"Of course it's never easy to abandon our old misconceptions and accept fresh ideas. Scientists bitterly attacked Galileo when he proved that the Leaning Tower of Pisa was a pendulum. They pooh-poohed Darwin's revolutionary notion that mankind is descended from the beagle. They laughed themselves sick at Edison's light bulb, as they will at any brilliant idea eons ahead of its time."

John Sladek, 'Space Shoes of the Gods'

The logic that controls the action of the following suite of linked tales isn't always the logic of everyday life; sometimes it's the logic of word association instead. Don't be dismayed or daunted. Step right inside!

TABLE OF CONTENTS

AN INCONVENIENT FRUIT

It is unknown how Thornton Excelsior obtained the peach that destroyed the world by flooding it with juice. He simply doesn't remember; the catastrophe was so immensely unexpected that it wiped his memory clean. He sat on his porch on a rocking chair and bit into the flesh of the fruit. And that was that.

Once the restraining skin of the peach was broached, the juice inside exploded outwards. The pressure of the spurting liquid jettisoned the fruit out of his grasp and it soared over the horizon and into the sea. The waves lapped themselves like cats made of milk. If he hadn't been sitting on a rocking chair the recoil would have killed him.

The juice spread across the surface of the ocean. Already the slick was larger than a province, a state, a federation. Thornton was aghast; it's not something that I recommend, being aghast, but you are welcome to try for yourselves. Sweet sticky juice rising inexorably, pouring over dykes and into flood plains. Inundation!

Presidents, kings and generals pointed the finger at him. They made an extra long finger by welding iron tubes together and poked him with it. He recoiled and hid under a table; but the steadily rising liquid forced him up the stairs and finally into his attic. The hollow finger followed him. Then it spoke; a voice vibrated out of it.

"Thornton, old son, don't worry about a thing. Those presidents, kings and generals are superfluous and will come to a sticky end. But I have taken a fancy to you and I will save you. I command you to build an ark, a vessel that can sail the tide of juice and keep you alive until the crisis is over - but this ark mustn't be made of wood or fibreglass or other conventional shipbuilding materials. To surf a global juice surge, only one substance is proper: planks of frozen clotted cream! Do you hearken to me, Thornton Excelsior?"

"Yes, yes! But who are you?"

"I am Zesto, the God of Fruit. Do what I command and all will be well. After forty days, give or take a month, the juice will recede and the ark will settle on solid ground. Then you may rebuild civilisation from scratch, or if not from scratch from itch. You may also found a religion in my name."

"Must I take one pair of every beast?"

"Animals on a ship made of clotted cream… Don't be silly!"

Thornton constructed his ark and it floated on the juice without sinking. The voice that lived in the tube never came back, not even when there was a violent storm. But Rosie O'Gassy said, "What the hell am I doing in this paragraph? I've never even existed as a character before." And Thornton Excelsior answered with a smile:

"You don't expect me to save humanity on my own?"

He was the first of the dessert fathers. His ark went rancid a long time ago, so there's no point looking for it; but I won't stop you if you insist. And Zesto put a giant banana in the sky to symbolise his promise that the world would never again be drowned in juice. There's a pot of yoghurt at the end of it, supposedly.

As for the presidents, kings and generals: they were impeached.

THE MAZE

Someone must have been telling the truth about Franz K, for one morning he found himself transformed into a literary giant. He was seated at his desk and when he lifted his head he could see his immense reputation stretching into the future ahead of him, lying on its back and waving its limbs in the air. But in fact he was prevented from looking.

I am a man of great wealth and dubious taste; I commissioned a special copy of K.'s *Complete Works* in one volume, with pages like bedsheets and letters the size of human ears. Then I went into the maze and pretended to read it. At the very centre.

While I was there I used my mobile telephone to call an ambulance. "My name is Thornton Excelsior." I said.

"There's nothing we can do about that, sir."

"I'm having a heart attack!" I cried.

"Stay calm. Help is on its way. Where are you?"

"The maze. Hurry. Ugh!"

Imagine the fuss as they tried to reach me in there, rushing through the entrance without a map, for maps of the maze are a closely-guarded secret, all in a group, two men holding a stretcher, the others with medical equipment of various kinds, defibrillators and similar machines, stethoscopes swinging from necks! At first they stayed together: then one man went the wrong way, broke off from the mass, lost himself down the branching conduits of a confusion transmuted from the abstract into the real. First one man, then more.

I listened to the muffled, diverging shouts.

Occasionally two separated voices would approach each other, seem to come together and merge; but in reality they were passing along parallel paths, destined never to meet but to split apart again. I chuckled to myself and slowly opened the cover of the vast book on the ground where I had placed it. No one may gain easy admittance to the centre of the maze and yet it is there for everyone. It exists for you.

I had flirted with the idea of combusting spontaneously. But then it would be firemen who came to my futile rescue instead of medics - and their hoses would show them the way out again, like the ball of string that every wise man takes with him into a labyrinth. Plus I had no clue how to combust in that manner.

Footsteps around the corner. Someone had found the correct route by chance alone. I hopped inside the book and lay flat: a space had been excavated within, like one of those books that hide whisky bottles. I closed the lid of my literary coffin just as my rescuers reached the centre of the maze. Two voices above the humming.

"There's no one here! Mr Excelsior, where are you?"

I grimaced as the other voice said, "Why is this gigantic book vibrating? Open it and look inside!"

The first did so. "Like a dog," he said.

"No, not like that. Much more like a condemned prisoner."

"Yes, in a penal settlement."

The letters were the size of human ears but the tails of some of them were tipped with needles. The text of my punishment was etched on my body, a new tale. I still quivered but I was already dead. So how am I able to write anything now? Because *this* story is the fatal text. One death sentence after another. My book was a special copy indeed, a remarkable piece of apocryphal apparatus.

HATSTANDS ON ZANZIBAR

In olden days hats were much more common than they are now. It seemed that everybody wore at least one. So plentiful were hats in general that the entire continent of Africa was needed to accommodate all the hatstands in existence; but now only one small island is necessary. Such is the decline in hat usage!

There was a knock on the door, soft and flabby, then again, bony and sharp. Thornton Excelsior opened it and blinked at the tall man who said, "Unintentional smiles."

"I beg your pardon?" replied Thornton.

"Have you ever smiled unintentionally at anyone and regretted it? Have you ever beamed at somebody you recognise in the street and then remembered, too late, you aren't supposed to like that person? Your smile was an unthinking reflex, in other words; and you bitterly curse yourself for giving it, and wish you could take it back?"

"What does that have to do with hatstands?" asked Thornton.

"Nothing, nothing. The hatstands story wasn't really going anywhere, so I decided to change it quickly. I'm glad I did, and you'll be glad too when you realise exactly what I'm offering. A rod."

Thornton continued to blink rapidly. "A rod?"

"Yes, a fishing rod that can catch all those unintentional smiles and reel them back! How about that?"

Thornton examined the object in question. "It's rather thick for a fishing rod," he said, "and a bit heavy too. I'm not sure whether I ought to trust you or not. I don't even know your name! And yet if it truly does what you claim—"

The tall man grinned. "Legitimus Blarney at your service. To be honest, that rod was made out of a redundant hatstand, thus proving there *is* a connection with the opening paragraph."

Thornton rubbed his chin. "I'm a man of great wealth and dubious taste, so it won't hurt too much if I take a chance on your product and it doesn't work. What is your asking price?"

11

The terms of the deal were earnestly discussed and the transaction was finally completed with a handshake. Mr Blarney departed and Thornton closed the door after him; then he climbed the stairs to the highest room of his house, and once there he opened the window and made his first cast. Almost immediately there was a bite.

He reeled with all his strength and soon enough discovered a hat impaled on the hook. "Bah!" sulked Thornton, convinced he had merely deprived some anachronistic but essentially innocent pedestrian of adequate headgear. But when he turned his catch over he saw a long-lost unintentional smile, one of his own, nestled at the bottom.

Hats are caves; smiles are bats.

As the days passed he soon amassed a sizeable collection of these smiles. Every evening he fished for an hour or two from that elevated window and rarely did he cast in vain. Then his luck changed; it became harder and harder to hook a smile. "But this is a good thing," he told himself, "for it means I have retrieved the vast majority of those smiles I never really wanted to bestow in the first place!"

He decided to melt them all down in a saucepan and turn them into a single ingot in a mould. Once it had cooled he would throw it into a lake together with the fishing rod. He vowed to be more careful with his mouth in future, keeping it tight-lipped when he encountered someone he didn't like.

When the ingot was ready he took it to the park and hurled it into the depths. It was still warm but it didn't hiss as it sank into the slime of the lakebed. As for the hatstand: it refused to submerge itself but merely floated like a minute hand on the clock face of its own ripple. Thornton wiped his hands on his trousers.

"Never again will I waste my evenings fishing for smiles!"

He turned to leave, wondering how many decades or centuries it would take for the ingot to decay down there, and on the way back home he felt satisfied and confident. But on the last street corner before he reached his house he almost collided with a man coming the other way. Thornton glanced at his face. Legitimus Blarney!

Before he could scowl at the tall fellow, Thornton realised to his dismay that he had already smiled instead. Casually, unthinkingly, reflexively, he had smiled an unintentional smile.

Mr Blarney had a quiver suspended over one shoulder; it was full of hatstands. "Plenty of rods left if you need another. I import them, you see, from a distant island."

Thornton Excelsior hurried away, hands over his ears.

Hats are dinosaurs; smiles aren't.

THE PORCELAIN PIG

Did I ever tell you the tale of the two explorers who discovered a gigantic porcelain pig in the jungles of Yuckystan? They climbed to the top of it and had an adventure that turned into a riddle. I don't think I did tell you about this, partly because I've never met you before; and also because I'm making it up as I go along. Making it up off the top of my head! But that doesn't mean it's not true. As for tops of heads: mine is perfectly smooth and sealed and doesn't feature a slot.

Yuckystan is a remote and inhospitable land and nobody knows much about the ancient civilisation that thrived there in the dim and distant past. So dim and distant was that past, in fact, that the people were required to go everywhere with powerful lamps on the ends of long poles. If they didn't do this, they tended to blunder into the margins of this paragraph and beget bruises on their brows and noses. How fortunate we are to live in a bright future where artificial illumination is needed only at night!

The names of the two explorers were Hogwash and Bum Note. They were an intrepid and valiant pair and already responsible for a number of astounding discoveries. Hogwash had explored Aplantis, the sunken vegetable continent, and charted the Awful Anguished Alcoves of the Alliteration Nation. Bum Note had explored his own sexuality in a Soho nightclub. Together they were a formidable team and on their very first joint expedition they even sneaked across the borders of Nullity itself and discovered the source of the Nil.

"Tell them about Wearyland too, won't you?"

Excuse me. That was Hogwash requesting that I inform the reader out there about the time he realised the landscape he was crossing was so heavily eroded that it was literally worn out: he encountered a *yawning* chasm. Even geology has a right to be tired! I went to Wearyland myself once, searching for a mythical mud monster. After many weeks I found it too, and wrote a report about it. I delivered my report on the mud monster to the committee of the Eldritch Explorers' Club but it just didn't wash.

"And what about NoNoLand? Don't forget that one!"

Now Bum Note is trying to get in on the act and create

another digression, but I won't be too hard on him and in fact I'll do what he asks and mention the occasion when they visited a micronation so small it was occupied entirely by the embassies of other countries with no territory left for itself. I haven't been there myself yet. By the way, I don't think we've been properly introduced. My name is Thornton Excelsior and I'm a tack of all jades, a sharper but greener version of the familiar jack.

So. The two explorers in Yuckystan... They hacked their way through the tangled vegetation of the rainforest with hire purchase machetes and sweated in the humidity like tightly gripped overripe fruits. Then they burst into a clearing and saw the pig. Thirty feet or more it towered above them. What could it be? The statue of a snuffling god? They used a grapple and a length of rope to get to its summit. In the very centre they discovered a narrow slot that dropped into the hollow interior of the thing. Hogwash was astounded.

"Why, it's nothing more than a grossly magnified piggybank!"

Bum Note cried, "But what's it for?"

"Saving monumental pennies," guessed Hogwash, "no doubt."

"They must have been a frugal people who built it, a civilisation of skinflints. I wonder if there's any spare change left inside? It's too dark to see very far down but if—"

"Look out, Bum Note!" shouted Hogwash.

But his warning came too late. The other explorer had leaned over too far and was in the act of falling headfirst into the slot. Hogwash lurched forward, grabbed one of Bum Note's ankles and managed to pull him out. But this feat of heroism so unbalanced Hogwash that he tumbled into the slot and disappeared. Bum Note heard the sickening thud of his body as it landed and all the bones inside it broke. There was also the sound of vast clanking pennies deep in the belly of the pig. Hogwash had sacrificed his own life in order to rescue his friend!

Bum Note climbed down and erected a small memorial by the side of the loathsome but financially astute edifice. Then he left Yuckystan and never returned. He gave a lecture at the Eldritch Explorers' Club that was attended by nearly every member. At the end of his talk he declared himself happy to answer questions about the expedition, including those primarily concerned with the dreadful fate of Hogwash. But the main question that everyone in the audience wanted to ask couldn't be answered at all.

Which of the two explorers was saved?

MAD MARCH STYLIST

An ancient forest in a forgotten valley. The sky was an intense blue with no clouds at all. A solid weight of heat pressed down on the trees, but no leaf stirred. The force was static.

"Your roots are showing," said an elm.

"Not again!" sighed an oak.

"You ought to go along to the salon," said the elm.

"But it's so expensive!"

"True, but you might as well get them done properly."

The oak uprooted itself and walked along the road towards the town. It was passed several times by vehicles but not one stopped to give it a lift, even though it held out a branch with a twig like an upraised thumb. The age of hitchers was dead and gone.

It reached the town in the late afternoon. The sun was less intense but the heat was still strong. Then the oak realised that it hadn't asked the elm to recommend a particular salon. So it simply went into the very first one it saw and, creakingly, took a seat.

Another customer, a human, was sitting on an adjacent chair. "Do you like this?" she asked suddenly.

"I don't know. What is it?" replied the oak.

"A cloud on a stick."

"What's the point of that?"

"It's the opposite of an umbrella, silly!"

"What happens when it blows inside out in a powerful wind? I guess the raindrops fly upwards?"

"I don't know. I've only just acquired it. Sassafras tells me that they'll be all the rage soon, what with the drought and all. Everyone will carry a cloud on a stick of their own."

"Who is Sassafras?" wondered the oak.

"I am!" From a hole in the wall appeared a creature with amazingly long ears. It twitched its nose, examined the oak from every conceivable angle. "A velveteen jacket, corduroy trousers, satin shirt and perhaps a bowler hat. That's my estimation."

The oak was flabbergasted. "What's going on? You're a giant

16

rabbit! Why are you putting clothes on me? I'm not a mannequin! I'm a tree. I don't want a silk cravat, thanks."

"A rabbit? No, no, I'm not one of those…"

"Stop clothing me, please!"

"This is a hare-dresser's, that's why. I'm the hare and I'm dressing you. What else did you expect, coming here? A blue paisley waistcoat as well, I think, and maybe green gloves…"

The oak returned to its home in the middle of the night. The elm was still awake and said, "Those trousers…"

"What about them?" demanded the oak.

"They're flares and too long."

"Yes, but they cover up my roots nicely…"

There was a long pause.

The elm asked, "Meet anyone interesting in town?"

The oak nodded. "A human female. She had a cloud on a stick. Told me her name was Mrs Excelsior, the wife of Thornton Excelsior. I think we could try making our own."

"Hawthorn Excelsior, did you say?"

"Thornton. Not a tree."

There was an even longer pause.

The elm said, "This story is too weak to be published."

"What story?" asked the oak.

"The one we're in right now. It should never have been written. I'd say it's a failure even as flash fiction."

"What's that?" asked the oak.

"A type of short story under one thousand words in length. But there's no need to worry, we're not going in any book. Not unless the author of this text is an incurable lunatic."

The oak considered this. "Flash fiction? Are you are sure that doesn't refer to the marks that look like writing after a bolt of lightning has struck a solid object on the ground?"

"Yes, I'm completely sure. It's what I said it is."

"How long is the story now?"

"624 words, not including the title. Or this sentence."

"And what about now?"

"Thirteen words more than before. 637."

"Is that the grand total?"

17

"Well, it was." The elm sighed and shook its boughs. "I'm going to bed now. So no more questions!"

"But I'll never be able to get to sleep unless—"

"676!" snapped the elm.

TEARS OF THE MUTANT JESTERS

Mr Thornton Excelsior replaced his favourite book on the special shelf of a small bookcase that stood in a secret alcove in a corner of his bedroom. He turned off the light, climbed between the sheets and experienced a full night's sleep instantly, for he had to move this story along quickly and it wasn't acceptable to waste paragraphs describing snores and dribbles. But his dreams were troubled and he thought he heard desperate cries coming from the region of the hidden alcove.

When he awoke, Dawn was breaking. He heard her smashing cups and plates in the kitchen. He got out of bed, wrapped himself in a robe, took a yawn with him and went to berate her.

"Good morning, sir! Sleep well?" she asked.

"Yes, I suppose so," he sighed.

"Was your paragraph comfortable enough, sir?"

"Thank you, Dawn, it was. But—"

"But what? That's a mighty fine yawn you have with you. Shall I slot a slice of toast into it right away, sir?"

"I've told you before how unnecessary it is to make breakfast for me. I can't afford to replace the crockery."

"Glue the shards back together later, I will, sir."

"Very well. Insert toast now."

She did so. He munched. Then he frowned and said, "What exactly are you doing here anyway? I never agreed to employ you as my housemaid. Before you smuggled yourself into my home dressed as a parcel of books, I was happy with my studious isolation. That's a fact. So don't you think it would be better if you went away?"

"Honestly no, sir, I don't, sir, as it happens, sir."

There was no answer to that.

Thornton drifted back to his bedroom in order to get properly dressed. While he was rummaging in the wardrobe for a suitable shirt, there was a howl from the alcove, a cry of pain. He went to investigate and found that his favourite book had mysteriously shifted position during the night. For no logical reason, its spine jutted further than the spines of its regimented fellows. This disruption of perfect order annoyed Thornton and he sought to rectify the discrepancy immediately.

With the tip of a fussy finger he pushed the book back into place, until it was flush with every other volume in the line, but this contact produced a dramatic response. The book wailed and visibly winced. Something was hurting it. Thornton was concerned and touched the book again. Another outburst! Removing every edition that stood on either side of the afflicted tome and putting them carefully on the bed, he leaned forward to examine the ailing hardback with a critical eye.

Deprived of its support, the book toppled over.

Then it opened its own cover, groaning even more pitifully as it did so, and ejected a weird vomit. The cover closed again, the book shivered, and Thornton contemplated the discharge.

A clear fluid containing undigested words!

He rubbed his chin, bemused.

Tenderness in the cover, dizziness and nausea…

What could all this mean?

His favourite book was an anthology of horror stories that were mostly surreal and fantastical rather than conventional. It was called *Tears of the Mutant Jesters* and it had been edited by no less an authority than Sniffer Grunting. It contained almost one hundred tales in which the most absurd events took place; and yet there was a curious veracity to everything that was described therein. The stories were less about how the world actually is than how it sometimes *feels*.

Ignoring its shrieks and whimpers with difficultly, Thornton picked up the book, quickly carried it to his bedside table and laid it down. Then he opened it as gently as possible.

The anthology sobbed and shivered. Perhaps it thinks I'm torturing it, mused Thornton. He rapidly flipped the pages, his jaw jutting out further every minute, until it seemed his lower face would become a bookshelf of its own. After the final tale there was an appendix in which the editor had an opportunity to discuss surrealistic horror stories in general, to justify that somewhat sidelined subgenre.

Finally Thornton had the answer to the medical riddle. It was shocking news! The book had appendicitis…

"I must operate immediately!" he declared. He jumped up and went in search of a suitable sharp instrument.

By this time, Midday had arrived.

She opened the front door with her skeleton key, went into the kitchen, dropped her overfilled shopping bags on the worktop and started opening and shutting cupboard doors, putting away the groceries. Thornton sighed as he intercepted her. "Not you again!"

"Of course it's me again, sir. Who do you expect, sir?"

"I hoped you wouldn't appear."

"Oh ho, you're a right joker, sir, make no mistake. Every day I come to fill your cupboard with foodstuffs."

"I can't stand the things you buy, to be honest."

Midday hefted heavy tins in her paws. "What do you mean, sir? Cream of Throat Soup! Insolent Beans in Despicable Sauce! Runny Git and Oaf Curry! Roughly Mashed Eyebrows! What finer fare might a gentleman of sustained reputation find anywhere?"

"Very well. Continue restocking my larder."

She did so. He watched. Then he frowned and said, "What exactly are you doing here anyway? I never agreed to employ you as my housemaid. Before you smuggled yourself into my home dressed as a can of thumbs, I was happy with my studious isolation. That's a fact. So don't you think it would be better if you went away?"

"Honestly no, sir, I don't, sir, as it happens, sir."

There was no answer to that.

Thornton rummaged among the cutlery for his sharpest knife. Once he found it, he went back to the bedroom. His favourite book was still crying and quivering. "Sorry, old friend," he said. He turned to the Appendix and saw how inflamed and incomprehensible it was. It must be removed now. He knew that delay could be fatal.

In his many decades as a bibliophile, this was the most serious case he had encountered. Earlier crises among his extensive collection had been due to relatively minor ailments, weak viral or fungal infections, nothing that rest and a positive critical review couldn't put right. He thought about those incidents and smiled wistfully.

One of his rarest monographs, *The Dionysian Artificers* by Hippolyto Joseph da Costa, had suffered from Athlete's Footnotes. And a Villiers de L'Isle-Adam book had become allergic to its own bookmark. A smearing of yoghurt had cured the first problem and a ribbonectomy had remedied the second. They were trivial cases.

21

Nothing to compare with this new disaster…

Poor suffering horror anthology!

Thornton began to perspire in empathy.

Wasting no more time on nostalgia, he cut out the entire Appendix and cast it aside. It was bloated and disgusting. The book screamed during the operation, but it was over in seconds.

"There!" cried Thornton to himself.

He mopped his brow. He used a mop with a curved handle to do this, a handle so curved it went away and came back almost immediately. As for the book, it had lost consciousness.

Probably a mercy, Thornton mused. He was gentle with it, replacing it on the shelf with extreme tenderness.

He leafed through the dismembered pages, the old enigma vibrating in his soul. What was the purpose of an Appendix? They seemed to serve no function. The orthodox opinion was that they had withered over the ages, growing smaller with each subsequent edition. Were they really vestigial echoes of a time when books ate grass?

The afternoon passed in futile contemplation of this question. Finally, it grew too late for further ponderings. Dusk was sweeping the land. With a resigned sigh, Thornton went out to apprehend her. She had swept clean most of the landscape between his house and the horizon and many of his favourite features were no longer there.

"Is it really necessary for you to do this?" he asked.

She shouldered her massive broom. "Yes, sir, I believe so, sir. Mustn't give mountains a chance to breed, sir."

"But I enjoyed looking at those peaks, Dusk!"

"Ranges are just clutter, sir."

He turned and walked back to his house. She followed him inside. Her broom knocked over an antique vase.

"That's not an ordinary ornament!" Thornton gasped.

This was a fact. It was also a robot.

With a pointed metal beard.

Dusk covered her mouth and said, "Oops!"

Thornton watched it fall. Then he frowned and said, "What exactly are you doing here anyway? I never agreed to employ you as my housemaid. Before you smuggled yourself into my home disguised as a hot geyseroo, I was happy with my studious isolation. That's a fact. So don't you think it would be better if you went away?"

"Honestly no, sir, I don't, sir, as it happens, sir."

There was no answer to that.

"What's a geyseroo?" asked the vase.

"It's like a geyser but hops around on two legs and has a pouch to keep baby xaratans in," said Thornton.

"What are xaratans?" wondered the vase. It attempted to stand but the plunge had damaged one of its gyroscopes. This was bad news. Once, not so long ago, it had entertained secret notions of taking over the world. No one knew that its real name was Ming the Merciless Vase. Its schemes of global conquest now had to be shelved.

Just like books recovering from surgery...

"Xaratans look like islands," explained Thornton, "but they are organic beings that drift about the oceans."

"I want to be an island in my next life," opined the vase.

"That's selfish," sniffed Thornton.

"Hey, there are two other housemaids in the kitchen! That's not right. I thought I was exclusive!" cried Dusk.

"You say that every day," pointed out Thornton.

Ming the Merciless Vase called after them from the hallway, "Anyone willing to help me up? A spider is about to scuttle inside my head. That's not nice, believe me. Too late now!"

Thornton sighed again. "Another fraught day."

"Fraught with what?" asked Dusk.

"With fraughts mainly."

"Oh those. I see."

"And with horrors too. Many horrors. Surreal horrors, but they are still horrific, at least in part."

Thornton drifted through the kitchen to the back door. He opened it and passed through into the garden. Beyond the low fence the world still existed right to the horizon. The removal of the mountains had exposed the steppe on the other side. A pack of books was feasting there but at this distance it wasn't possible to see what they were devouring. Thornton grew excited. What if it was grass?

He might have discovered genuinely wild books: a pure strain that had never evolved into shelf-sitters. He fetched his telescope and raised it to his eye. Now he could read the titles on the spines. Each volume was a single author collection and every author was represented in *Tears of the Mutant Jesters*. Then he turned his attention to what sprawled beneath them and sighed in disappointment.

Nothing special. Just the cadaver of a librarian.

THE PARADOXICAL PACHYDERMS

The greatest explorers in the world regard the entire planet as home, so it logically follows that when they get lost they get lost in their own homes. Mediocre explorers also get lost in their own homes; I know of one case, Plucky Ruckus by name, who took three years to locate the source of the leak that had flooded his living room; he followed the banks of the stream and finally discovered that it came from his bathroom, but on the stairs he was kidnapped by a tribe of cannibals and eaten for supper. Fortunately for him, there were plenty of leftovers, so in the morning he was able to stagger the remainder of the journey.

As for the very worst explorers, they don't know *how* to get lost. They haven't even discovered that knowledge yet. They wander aimlessly over various kinds of landscapes, between the peaks of spitting volcanoes and through shopping malls, into the houses of other people and out the other side, shouting, "Are we not there yet?"

Nobody ever gives an answer to that question.

My name is Thornton Excelsior and I am one of the administrators of the Eldritch Explorers' Club, which is a society dedicated to totally weird adventure and utterly implausible travel. My official task is to accurately document the exploits of our active members. It's not a full-time post but only one of my many posts. I have so many posts I may be described as a fence; however, that appellation seems to attract the interest of the police, I can't guess why, so I tend not to use it.

Every year, at our annual general meeting, I am required to read aloud the reports I have made of the most notable journeys of our members. In the expectant hush of our hallowed trophy-cluttered Anecdote Chamber, I stand on the podium and regale my worthy colleagues with ludicrous but factual accounts of voyages undertaken; and in many cases of explorers undertaken too, for not everyone who embarks alive comes back that way. In fact they often don't come back at all and there isn't a skeleton to measure for a coffin, or even a loose ribcage or foot for the undertakers to dress tastefully in a waistcoat or nice shoe before proper burial. But those are the risks associated with exploration.

Last year I had to recite aloud the obituary of Whymper Bowman, an explorer renowned for climbing mountains in reverse. His technique was ingenious and silly: he would jump out of an aircraft and parachute onto the summit of a peak, and from there he would climb down to the bottom headfirst. He called this method 'unconquering' and claimed it was less patronising and imperialistic than making a normal ascent. In this manner he unconquered Ben Nevis on his eighteenth birthday, Mont Blanc when he was twenty and Aconcagua when he was thirty, progressing to higher and higher altitudes. On his fortieth birthday he successfully unconquered Mount Everest. After that, there was only Rum Doodle, which at 40,000½ feet should be better known than it is.

When he finally reached the base of Rum Doodle, touching the ground with the crown of his head, Whymper Bowman formally announced his retirement; but destiny had other plans for him. A local porter, who later turned out to be a yeti in disguise, casually mentioned that in the legends of his own people there was an even higher mountain to the north; known only as Madness Mountain, it was higher than Rum Doodle some of the time, because it kept changing its height according to its moods. It was a completely insane geographical feature.

Mr Bowman soon became obsessed with it and made preparations to add it to his impressive list of unconquests. Every time he was asked why he wanted to 'climb' an insane mountain upside-down, he gave the same answer, "Because it's not all there."

That was his last adventure. True, he successfully parachuted onto the summit of Madness Mountain; but at that moment it chose to quadruple its altitude and it rose out of the atmosphere, suffocating Mr Bowman in the freezing vacuum of space. The yeti chuckled at this, rubbed his hairy palms in cryptozoological glee and carved another notch into the handle of his walking stick, which was the tusk of a mammoth. Yetis don't like explorers very much because they often smell of mint cake, which is the most loathsome odour to mythical beasts.

So much for Whymper Bowman! He was daft but brave. That's worth something, isn't it?

The same can't be said for a pair of fellows who almost certainly are the worst explorers I have ever encountered. Sometimes I suspect they have been sent by a higher supernatural agency to mock the pretensions of the Eldritch Explorers' Club. Yet they are likeable enough and there's never any question of revoking their membership.

Hogwash and Bum Note are their names. Maybe you are familiar with their exploits in the dense jungles of Yuckystan? One of them fell into a giant piggybank that had been erected centuries earlier by a previously unknown civilisation; it was a long fall and there was no escape from the inside, but once you fall into a piggybank you are 'saved', so everything turned out fine in the end. It has been rumoured that interest was earned on the saving; but I don't believe that.

On another occasion, they declared their intention to climb the most notable 'peak' in England; that doesn't sound like so fine an achievement until you realise that they were very bad at spelling and were referring to Mervyn Peake. I gather the attempt annoyed that great writer and he kept brushing them off. What a *Gormenghastly* pun that was! It made me *Titus Groan*! All the same, it really happened.

Not long ago, last week in fact, Hogwash turned to Bum Note. "We have explored much of the physical world together, so don't you think it's time we explored a figure of speech instead?"

"What do you have in mind?" wondered Bum Note.

"Our sexuality. We haven't explored that properly yet, have we?" said Hogwash. Bum Note considered this.

"I explored my own once, in a Soho nightclub."

"Indisputable, but we didn't explore it together. That was merely *your* sexuality. What about *our* sexuality?"

"Fair enough. There's a bus to Brighton in half an hour."

"Let's get on it!" cried Hogwash.

"Going to Brighton is exactly what we need."

"Yes. Brighton's just the ticket!"

"Really? That's a big ticket," said Bum Note.

"It's another figure of speech," explained Hogwash patiently. "We'd hardly pay for a trip to Brighton with Brighton itself, would we? For one thing, we'd never get it on the bus."

"We wouldn't need a bus if we already had it."

"True, true," conceded Hogwash.

"Let's go to Brighton! To Brighton!" chortled Bum Note.

"Ready when you are, chum!"

And that's what they did. When they reached Brighton they wandered the quaint streets at random; they visited the Royal Pavilion and went to stand on the pier. Finally they sat on a bench in the light of the setting sun and Bum Note sighed with dismay.

"We haven't even *located* our sexuality yet, let alone explored it. I bet we're overlooking something obvious."

"I'm overlooking the beach," said Hogwash blithely.

"Yes, but there's no merit in just exploring a beach. We must be doing something wrong. I wonder what?"

"Maybe we need to *find* our sexuality before we can *explore* it? If we don't have it at our fingertips, we won't be able to plant our flag in it. By the way, did you bring the flag?"

"Of course I did," replied Bum Note. "I've got a nice pole to run it up. But how can we find our sexuality?"

"By hunting for it," suggested Hogwash.

"But we don't have a hunting license," said Bum Note. "Also, I regard hunting as an immoral activity."

"So do I, as it happens."

"Why don't we trap it instead, humanely?"

"Good idea. Let's do that!"

"But how?" pondered Bum Note.

"Maybe we should hire an exotic dancer as bait?"

"It's worth a try, I guess…"

The task of finding an exotic dancer for hire in Brighton was easy, too easy perhaps; but anyway, she stood in front of them and undulated in the moonlight. Hogwash and Bum Note sat rigid on their bench, side-by-side, knees touching, like statues. They stared without comment. Hours passed, but they knew that trapping figures of speech could be a tricky business. At last, just before dawn, it happened…

"There it is. Our sexuality!" squealed Hogwash.

"Plant the flag!" cried Bum Note.

"You've got it. Hurry!" blurted Hogwash.

"Watch out! Here goes!"

With a wild primeval howl, Bum Note thrust the point of the flagpole into the very centre of their sexuality. The exotic dancer ceased her sultry gyrations and covered her mouth with a hand. It was the most shocking thing she had seen in her career.

"Ouch!" screamed Hogwash and Bum Note.

It took an entire troupe of dedicated doctors to get the flagpole out and eighty metres of cotton to bandage the wounded sexuality. Hogwash and Bum Note walked with a synchronised limp for a decade afterwards. That kind of injury heals very slowly. If you don't believe me, try planting a flag in your own sexuality sometime.

I've already mentioned that my name is Thornton Excelsior. A few days ago I was woken by my pet ghost. I didn't mention that I had a pet ghost, did I? Well, I do; and it woke me up.

"But the sun hasn't risen yet," I protested.

The ghost floated higher above my bed and said, "There are strange sounds coming from the garden. I think you should go and investigate. I don't want to go. I'm frightened."

Grumbling, I dressed and went out in my slippers.

And I saw a remarkable sight.

Miniature elephants, a herd of them, were grazing on my lawn. There were also some tiny rhinos and hippos. Emboldened by my presence, my ghost came up behind me and peered timidly over my shoulder. "Maybe they aren't really miniature elephants, rhinos and hippos; perhaps they are normal-sized but far away," it said.

"My lawn isn't that big," I pointed out reasonably.

"Good point," murmured my ghost.

I kneeled down for a closer look. One of the elephants clambered onto the open palm of my right hand.

I lifted it higher and smiled. "These must be the fabled Paradoxical Pachyderms hitherto only spotted in the Bunlands," I remarked. But as I leaned forward, the little beast launched itself at me and stabbed my neck deeply with one of its sharp tusks.

"Yow!" I exclaimed.

"What's the matter?" asked my ghost. "Did somebody plant a flag in your sexuality?" His tone was ironic.

"Nope," I said simply.

I went back inside the house. The entry point of the miniature tusk was already swelling into a large boil.

Frowning, I regarded the potato that had been sitting in a saucepan on my stove for the past week. The problem was that the stove wasn't real; it was just a model made from matchsticks; and those matchsticks were all burned out; so there was no way of generating any heat from the device. I found cooking meals therefore difficult, impossible in fact. I hadn't tasted a cooked potato for many years.

Now I had an idea. I picked up the saucepan by its handle and moved it next to the swelling on my neck.

"What do you think you're doing?" asked my ghost.

"Bringing the potato to the boil," I said.

Before it was quite ready to eat, there was a knock at the door. So I put down the saucepan and went to answer it. Two figures stood there; one of them was a mirror image of the other, but I don't know which. Therefore it's impossible for me to describe them.

"I'm about to have my breakfast," I said.

"We won't keep you for long," they said. "We are the characters you have recently libelled most awfully."

"If my libel was substandard, I'll try again."

"We would prefer it if you didn't bother. I'm Hogwash and this is Bum Note and you depicted us as imbeciles. But we aren't like that at all; we're serious explorers and so we demand that you write a new piece about our particular brand of original heroism."

"What brand is that?" I asked tolerantly.

"Please don't play games with us. It's hard enough being fictional even when we are treated with respect; but when an author creates us just as a focus for puns and silly jokes... It's irresponsible, that's what it is, and we want a better story to appear in than this; or if you can't do that, then you should rewrite our parts in *this* tale."

"You must have confused me with someone else," I said. "My name is Thornton Excelsior and I only write factual reports on what daft explorers get up to. I never handle fiction."

They asked, "Who does the ghost belong to?"

"To me. He's my pet," I said.

"No, we mean who was he when he was alive…"

"I don't know," I admitted.

"Well, why don't you ask him?" they said.

I turned to my ghost and cried, "Who were you when you were alive? I assume this is just a formality…"

And the ghost replied, "My name is Hector Gloopbunny, and I was an explorer before I fell off the edge of the map. The impact killed me. The problem was that I unfolded the map on top of a magic carpet. Such a bad place to spread it out! The carpet was flying high at the time; so when I fell off, it was a very long way down. I was famous in my day but never a member of the Eldritch Explorers' Club."

"Did you land on something hard, Mr Gloopbunny?"

My pet ghost answered with a sigh, "Two rotten explorers who looked exactly like these two fellows here."

"Maybe they are the same pair?" I wondered.

"If so, they are ghosts like me. I killed them with the force of my fall. I recommend you try poking them with a finger. If the finger goes through, it'll be proof they are indeed spooks."

I didn't have the nerve to extend my own finger and do what my ghost recommended. I picked up a dictionary from a bookshelf and threw that at them instead, because it contained the word 'finger', as well as many other words, not all of them suitable for poking things with. The flesh of my visitors provided no resistance at all.

The dictionary went straight through and hit the wall.

They were spectres, both of them; explorers of the other side, the outer limits, the spirit worlds, and bad at it too.

Later, I went back into the garden and collected some of the miniature elephants and other creatures. I thought it might be nice to bring them indoors and play with them for a short period, to take my mind off the stress occasioned by life in general.

I had imprisoned Hogwash and Bum Note in bottles after compressing them first in ghost-proof bags. I thought it might be fun to introduce the elephants, rhinos and hippos into the same bottles. I'm not an especially nice person, in case you're wondering.

Then I noticed that among the pachyderms there was a miniature yeti. He was stalking a miniature mammoth. I reached out to snatch him up, but it turned out I had misjudged distance. Thanks to odd perspective, he was actually a full-sized yeti far away.

"My garden still isn't that big!" I protested.

My pet ghost floated onto my shoulder and perched there. "Clearly it is. You must have ordered an extension on credit when you realised you had two rare ghosts to sell as pets…"

He has a sharp business mind, that Hector Gloopbunny. I didn't miss the hint and I went back into the house to fetch the bottles. Then I set out on the long trek towards the yeti. One day I'll write up the account of this expedition for my own organisation.

After an hour of hard bargaining, I got a very good price for Hogwash and Bum Note. And the yeti was pleased by the transaction. He chuckled, rubbed hairy palms in cryptozoological glee and carved two extra notches into the handle of his walking stick.

I had already forcefed them on mint cake.

THE INTEGERS

No sooner had he died in a terrible accident than Thornton Excelsior expected to be told what to do next. There should be music, a celestial choir, the melodies of the spheres, and maybe a personal guide to smooth his passage to the other side, assuming some other side existed. But nothing of the sort happened. He was left alone, his soul now larger than his flattened body, and he blinked sadly at the steamroller as it continued on its way down the rutted road.

"The flesh is inside the ghost for once," he told himself, "and it's a reversal I don't much care for. I think I'll float just a little distance to the side and wait there instead."

And that's what he did. He positioned himself on the verge of the decaying highway, watching the steamroller compress the ruts until it vanished around a bend. He stood there until the sun went down.

"Some sort of help or clue would be appreciated," he grumbled.

The stars came out; an owl flapped almost silently above his head like a ghost, a ghost with feathers and a large head, a ghost in the exact shape of an owl, a ghost that *was* an owl in fact. Thornton hated similes and metaphors. The owl flapped through the night air like an owl. Like itself. Yes, that was better. He grimaced: he hated smiles too.

"No message for me, nothing," he sighed sadly.

Then it occurred to him that maybe the responsibility for making contact was his. He dropped to his knees in the grass and clasped his hands together in an attitude of prayer. His mind swirled with thoughts and images but all of them were vague or fractured and he was unable to formulate a clear question.

Finally he stuttered, "Hello?"

A dim crackling noise filled his ears: static electricity.

"Anyone there?" he mumbled.

A voice twanged inside his skull, in the ghostly echo of a skull that was more than an afterimage but less than a reflection. It was a polite but efficient female voice and it said, "There's no one available to deal with your soul at the present moment. Please hold."

"Hold what?" blurted Thornton, even though he knew the answer: his hands together. So he held them more tightly.

Strange xylophone music played inside his mind.

Hours passed in this manner.

The music was complex and atonal and seemed to be based on some abstruse mathematical pattern beyond Thornton's mental grasp. No phrase was repeated and he finally realised that the notes were predetermined by a scheme that involved exhausting an immensely large sequence of possibilities. Then at last the cycle was completed and it began again from the beginning. A psychosomatic cramp tormented his fingers.

"This is ridiculous. I've had enough of it!" he fumed.

But he remained on his knees, listening, waiting. And just as the first glimmer of dawn appeared on the eastern horizon, the music abruptly stopped and the female voice returned, cool and professional and so fluid that Thornton was unable to interrupt at any point. Not that a successful interruption would have done him any good: this female was purely automatic.

"If you are Jewish say the number 'one'; if you are Christian say 'two'; if you are Hindu say 'three'; if you are…" recited the voice, working its way through all the major and minor world religions. Thornton blinked. What was he? It was too late to convert to one of the monotheistic faiths: a postmortem conversion to those is invalid. He supposed he was a Buddhist. It seemed the most reasonable choice on offer.

"Eight!" he cried, for that was the number required.

The female voice fell silent for half a minute. Then it returned, brisk and emotionless. "If you wish to be reincarnated as a wolf say 'one'; as a bear say 'two'; as an ostrich say 'three'; as a weeping willow say 'four'; as a millipede say 'five'; as an octopus…"

Thornton listened carefully. The list went on and on.

"…as a dormouse say 'two hundred and thirty one'; as a swan say 'two hundred and thirty two'; as a…"

Having decided to wait to hear every single option, to be certain of not missing the best on offer, Thornton soon grew appalled at the sheer quantity of potential lifeforms. It seemed the woman intended to list every animal and plant in creation. Although it is bad manners for dead people to fall asleep, Thornton dozed off, still in a kneeling position. Then he snapped awake. It was midday and the landscape shimmered.

"…as a centaur say 'eighty million four hundred and nine thousand three hundred and sixty three'; as a unicorn…"

Thornton gasped. The female voice had reached mythical beings; so how long had he been asleep? Maybe the time was noon of some *other* day. With eternity before him, the loss of entire days meant nothing. But he was utterly exasperated with the entire procedure. Enraged, he opened his mouth as wide as he could and shouted:

"Ten squillion zillion trillion billion million and one!"

A purely random integer…

Disgusted with everything, he unclasped his aching hands and broke the connection; then he stood and stamped fake life back into his dead legs. He had always assumed that the administrative wheels of the afterlife would turn quickly, so the realisation that inefficiency was the basic rule beyond the grave was almost unbearable. In a fit of pique he vowed to remove himself from the system completely.

"I'll exist as a ghost forever," he told himself.

Why not? Why should he be forced to commit himself to the rules of any formal religion? He would surely be happier as a freelance spook, at liberty to drift wherever he liked, to enjoy himself afresh among his old haunts. He spread his arms like featherless wings and willed himself to rise and he felt no astonishment at all when the ground dropped away. This was the right choice after all…

"Much better than reincarnation!" he chortled.

The landscape far below became interesting as an object in its own right, without the need to relate it to a mental map of the territory. Among the network of narrow roads, a steamroller moved silently, possibly ending the lives of other unwary ramblers. Somehow Thornton knew that the man who drove the machine was Giddy Snark, the current chairman of the Flat Earth Society. That's what all members of the FES were required to do: drive around in steamrollers to promote their cause.

Thornton resisted the impulse to descend and scare the man. Such petty revenge was beneath him, metaphorically as well as literally. The beat of wings made him flinch. The owl that looked like a ghost in the shape of an owl was back. "Awake in the day! Did you have difficulty sleeping?" he called after it. And it shook its head in reply.

Then it was gone, but a feeling of amazement remained with Thornton and he wondered if the owl was a reincarnation of anyone he knew. A sudden dire thought struck him: what if the random number he had shouted actually stood for something?

Maybe 'ten squillion zillion trillion billion million and one' was the code for a terrible entity, a rhinoceros with a boot instead of a horn (a shoehorn?) or an inside-out monkey? What if he was reborn as a horrid spiderpus, an amalgam of giant spider and giant octopus! Fear disrupted his concentration; he had stopped rising but now he began to float in an easterly direction.

The sea sparkled on the horizon. It seemed to pull him.

He passed over a beach where a curious drama was taking place. A perfectly straight line of men and women thrusting out from the shore into the briny deeps. Thornton estimated that at least three hundred individuals were present. Three hundred! Yet another cursed integer: a number that stood for a weasel in the reincarnation lists.

Blinking, he realised he had misinterpreted the spectacle below. It wasn't a drama at all but an unplanned consequence of the dangerous currents in this part of the world. A sign on the beach proclaimed: DANGER! SWIM ONLY BETWEEN THE SAFETY FLAGS! The flags in question, half red and half yellow, were planted only the width of a single person apart. That explained the single file arrangement: the swimmers had no other choice.

Thornton continued to drift out to sea, his altitude dropping all the time. Seagulls glided below him; flying fish below those; and on the surface of the water itself came a wondrous boat, a golden skiff with a silver sail, steered by a naked helmsman with orange skin and a purple beard.

The angle of Thornton's descent was gentle enough to deposit him on the deck of the skiff with no more awkwardness than a man stepping down from a gangplank resting on the rails. Instead of passing through the boat and into the ocean, the ghost of the squashed man acted like an ordinary sailor. Clearly the skiff possessed the ability to hold his soul in place, some sort of magnetic attraction. He blinked in anticipation.

"Hello," said the helmsman in a crisp voice, "my name is π."

"π?" gasped Thornton in alarm.

"Not pi question mark. Just π. I'm the personification of that irrational number. I am responsible for circles. How do you do?"

"I can't complain," said Thornton.

"My question was just a courteous formality. I'm a messenger and I'm here to tell you to report to Divinopolis immediately."

"Divinopolis? What's that?"

"It's one of the major cities of Heaven," said π.

"How do I get there?"

"Straight up." And π pointed vertically with his free hand, grasping the tiller even more tightly with the other.

"Why should I obey you?" frowned Thornton.

"It's your duty. All the Cardinal Numbers have gathered to elect a new spiritual leader. Pope Integer the Infinite is due to make his first speech at $\sqrt{}$o'clock. You shouldn't be late for that! If you're late, you'll miss it and you have an obligation to attend. Hurry!"

"None of this has anything to do with me. I'm a ghost."

"No, you're not," said π.

Thornton was baffled. "What do you mean?"

"You were reincarnated earlier today. You asked for reincarnation and made your choice by shouting out a specific number and now you've got what you asked for. Indeed, you *are* what you asked for!"

"What is that?" rasped Thornton.

"A number. You have been reborn as a number."

Thornton trembled. "Which one?"

"Ten squillion zillion trillion billion million and one."

"The same number I shouted out aloud! It represented itself: what an incredible coincidence! I'm not a prime, by any chance? No, I can see that I'm not. I can *feel* it. Imagine me as a number! Ha ha! And I'm a Cardinal Number, you say? But what are they?"

"Cardinal Numbers include the natural numbers, which are the ordinary counting numbers, followed by the aleph numbers, which are all transfinite. You are a strange number but not an impossible one. All Cardinals are required in Divinopolis to attend the Pope's speech."

"Very well. I shall ascend there now."

"Straight up and turn left at the zenith. Go as fast as you can. It's imperative you arrive before the square root of o'clock."

Thornton Excelsior began to rise vertically into the sky like a rocket without a visible engine, rotating on his own axis for the purpose of generating stability, the sunlight glinting on his abstract hide. The helmsman below craned his head to follow his progress; as a consequence he collided with the line of swimmers, propelling them like a human javelin between the safety flags and onto the beach. They howled at this treatment.

"Oh dear! They are furious with me now," muttered π.

Thornton glanced down and cried, "How do you know that?" He had guessed rather than heard the helmsman's complaint. π shook his head slowly and answered sadly:

"Because they are very angry…"

"That sounds like a circular argument," objected Thornton.

"Of course," came the reply. "It's what I do. I'm responsible for circles of all kinds. I have a finger in every π. But let's not end with a pun! Give my regards to Pope Integer. Farewell!"

THE SHRUG

Many solar-powered slave drivers make light work. That's the saying. But Thornton Excelsior wasn't one of those; he was a man and fuelled himself with food and drink like you and me.

Sitting in a soft chair after filling himself right to the brim with human fuel he was faced with a dilemma. That last remaining chocolate cake on the plate. What ought he to do with it?

If he allowed it to go stale, his wife would be annoyed.

He didn't have a wife – yet.

So that's no excuse. He might have her one day.

And yet, if he crammed it into his mouth, the cake I mean, he would undoubtedly feel extremely nauseous and his health might be ruined. If that happened, he would probably never have a wife to congratulate him for not wasting it. Such a paradox.

What was the solution? What indeed!

He desperately needed advice.

And he got it, most unexpectedly. An angel materialised on his right shoulder and said, "Don't eat it."

An instant later, a devil appeared on his left shoulder.

"Stuff it in your gob," it urged.

Thornton Excelsior slowly considered both pieces of advice and tried to weigh them in his mind to determine which was the most profound. He planned to follow the heaviest. While waiting patiently for the imaginary scales to settle, he licked his lips. He had licked his own lips before, so he knew exactly what he was doing.

"Don't listen to *him*," warned the angel.

"*He's* the liar," said the devil.

Thornton blinked. The mental scales had now settled and were evenly balanced. Or were they? He thought he detected a slight bias in the devil's favour. He couldn't be sure and decided to interrogate the devil in order to arrive at a better-informed decision.

"Why do you think I should devour it?" he asked.

"Because it's fun," said the devil.

"How do you know that?" persisted Thornton.

The devil flicked his tail. "It's the final chocolate cake. You've already eaten too many of them. If you manage to cram this one into your mouth also, you will attain the status of a true glutton; and gluttony is wrong. It's a truism that wrong things are fun."

"I suppose so. And yet... I still have doubts."

"Put them aside," the devil said.

Thornton blinked. "I don't suppose you'd care to check your statement for me? Your claim that wrong things are fun, I mean. A second opinion on that would be very welcome, if it isn't too much trouble. Could you do that favour before I commit myself?"

The devil was bewildered. "How can I do that?"

"Consult a trusted source. Ask someone," said Thornton. "Surely you have access to a higher authority?"

"Ask me!" cried the angel.

"A *lower* authority, don't you mean?" said the devil.

"If you like," agreed Thornton.

"Ask me!" bleated the angel.

"Be quiet!" snapped Thornton and he flicked the angel off his shoulder and into a cobweb in the darkest corner of the cluttered room. A spider at once rushed out and sank its fangs into the angel, then bound it tight with a cocoon of silk. An unpleasant fate.

The devil shrugged. "I don't know what to do..."

Suddenly a tiny angel materialised on its right shoulder and said, "Tell him that wrong things *aren't* fun. Tell him about consequences to actions, about responsibility and duty."

But another devil appeared on the first devil's left shoulder. "Rubbish! That's just your opinion, not the truth."

"What would you know about such things?" cried the angel.

"Everything," snapped the devil.

An even smaller angel appeared on that devil's right shoulder. "Why are you so arrogant? Maybe you don't really know much at all. I think it may do you good to listen for once—"

"Don't waste your breath!" growled another devil that appeared on the devil's left shoulder. But an even smaller angel appeared on this devil's right shoulder and began berating him.

More and more angels and devils started materialising on shoulders. A tower was being constructed on Thornton's own shoulder that rapidly rose higher than the ceiling of the room that contained him; it went through the open skylight above and kept lifting into the sky, a sequence of ever smaller and shriller supernatural beings.

Thornton was aghast. "I never guessed that shoulder angels and devils had shoulder angels and devils of their own! The weight of the conflicting advice is crushing me into my chair..."

There was only one thing he could do to save himself.

He shrugged them all off.

Then he jumped up and went outside. Standing on the porch he had a nasty thought. He crouched down and touched the wooden boards with his fingers. Yes, they felt more like hard flesh than planks. He stood up straight again and cleared his throat.

He was standing on a giant's shoulder. He tried not to work out *which* shoulder, right or left; he refrained from bristling his horns or flapping his wings. He shut his eyes very firmly.

But the moment of panic passed quickly. Then he leaned over. "Go on, do it!" he whispered into the massive ear. "Grind his bones to make your bread. It's healthier than white flour. Honest!"

THE LONGEST NAME

They sent him to seek out the longest place name in the world. He started his quest in Wales, that peculiar country where the rain never stops, and it wasn't too long before he found himself in *Llanfairpwyllgwyngyllgogerychwyrndrobwllllandysiliogogogoch* on the island of Anglesey, where the druids once cavorted. He met an old man in a tavern who chuckled at his naivety for long minutes and then said:

"The name of this village is a trick, the fabrication of a crafty tailor in the previous century who wished to attract visitors. The tongue twister is a description and means 'St Mary's Church in the hollow of white hazel near a rapid whirlpool and the Church of St Tysilio near the red cave'. Be not deceived by appearances, my friend!"

"Call me Thornton."

"Why should I do that?"

"Partly because it's my name."

"That is a solid reason. Now let me tell you of another place in Wales with an even longer name. Few people are aware of its existence." And he whispered into the visitor's ear.

Thornton Excelsior was grateful for his advice.

He drank up and left the pub.

Heading south, it took him a few days of walking to reach an isolated station on a very obscure railway line that rejoiced, or palpitated, in the somewhat alarming name *Gorsafawddacha'idraigodanheddogleddollônpenrhynareurdraethceredigion*. There is a reference to 'dragon's teeth' amid that jumble, but he didn't know that then. There was nothing worth seeing there, but he lingered anyway.

The wind whipped his face, drying it slightly.

An old man appeared and said, "Are you here for the name? I thought as much! It's a long one, that's for sure; but I have sailed around the world and I can assure you that longer names exist elsewhere. You must journey far to locate them! Do you believe me?"

"I do," said Thornton, "because you look familiar."

"No, I don't. Never that…"

Thornton bowed his head. He realised that his quest was going to take a lot longer than he had anticipated.

41

He headed in a southerly direction and eventually wandered into a part of Wales so remote and grim that even the Welsh aren't aware of it. Near the grotesque village of Lladloh, choked by the undergrowth of the dense forest, stood the ruins of a long-extinct community that was once a mirror image of its neighbour, a weird reversal of that frightful anomaly; but this doesn't mean it was a pleasant place.

Thornton wandered among the shells of old buildings. They really did look like shells too: those of nightmarish gastropods. At last he found the signpost he had been looking for. It gave the name of the village as *Yrotssihtrofyllaicepseputiedamiesuacebseirotsrehtoymfoynaniraeppalliwegallivsihttahttbuodylsuoiresi*. No wonder the community imploded! While he was musing thus, there was a rustle.

"Good morning, I'm Russell," said a creaking voice.

Thornton turned and found himself facing another old man. Why was it always old men who materialised to give him advice? But he was polite enough and said, "Hello to you."

The old man waved a gnarled hand.

"Yes," he began, "my former village did have a monstrously elongated name, but there are others even longer elsewhere and beyond. That is why I'm waving this gnarled hand at you."

"Where did you find it?" asked Thornton.

The old man dropped the gnarled hand. "It was hanging on a tree. I do enjoy waving it about now and then."

"Thank you for sharing your wisdom, sir!"

And Thornton hastened away and didn't dare look back until the forest was far behind him. He kept going until he finally reached the coast; and in the old port of Tenby he went aboard a ship and sailed to distant lands, always seeking the longest place name.

In Massachusetts he discovered a lake called *Chargoggagoggmanchauuggagoggchaubunagungamaugg* but nothing longer than that in the rest of the American continent; and in New Zealand he visited *Taumatawhakatangihangakoauauotamateaturipukakapikimaungahoronukupokaiwhenuakitanatahu* and came away bewildered.

Always he was met by old men with advice...

At last, after many years of wandering, he returned to the site and the people from whence he had started out.

It was the clubhouse of the Eldritch Explorers' Club.

They interviewed him in a room that was spherical; and he stood at the bottom, where the southern pole might be, while they occupied a balcony set high up on the northern tropic line.

"Did you find the longest place name of all?" they asked.

Thornton Excelsior looked at them and he recognised the faces of all the old men who had approached him. There was Caradoc Weasel, Icarus Evans, Gamma-Ray Russell, Tonguewaggle Chipchop, Janus Cronk, Ork Warder, Unshackle Erneston and others.

"I did better than that," Thornton said defiantly.

"What do you mean?" they cried.

"Wherever I went, I dropped a letter from my pocket. When I crossed the ocean these letters sank onto the seabed; but always they were linked to the letters that went before and all those that came after. Eventually the string of letters circled the entire globe."

"And what of that?" his interrogators demanded.

"I created a new place in the process," replied Thornton, "and certainly it has the longest name in the world. It's such a long name that it encircles the planet and comes back to the beginning again; indeed it forms a loop that is infinite. When you set off for that place, how can you ever know if you have reached it? Simultaneously you will be there and not there. That is my achievement. Judge me accordingly."

"Tell us the name of this place," they insisted.

"Are you sure you want to hear it?"

They nodded in assent.

So Thornton took a deep breath, the deepest that has ever been taken, and spoke the following word:

Theysenthimtoseekoutthelongestplacenameintheworldhestarted-hisquestinwalesthatpeculiarcountrywheretherainneverstopsanditwasnt-toolongbeforehefoundhimselfinllanfairpwyllgwyngyllgogerychwyrndrob-wllllandysiliogogogochontheislandofangleseywherethedruidsoncecavort-edhemetanoldmaninatavernwhochuckledathisnaivetyforlongminute-sandthensaidthenameofthisvillageisatrickthefabricationofacraftytai-lorinthepreviouscenturywhowishedtoattractvisitorsthetonguetwisterisad-escriptionandmeansstmaryschurchinthehollowofwhitehazelneararapid-whirlpoolandthechurchofsttysilioneartheredcavebenotdeceivedbyap-pearancesmyfriendcallmethorntonwhyshouldidothatpartlybecauseitsmy-namethatisasolidreasonnowletmetellyouofanotherplaceinwaleswith-

anevenlongernamefewpeopleareawareofitsexistenceandhewhisperedin-
tothevisitorsearthorntonexcelsiorwasgratefulforhisadvicehedrankupan-
dleftthepubheadingsouthittookhimafewdaysofwalkingtoreachanisolated-
stationonaveryobscurerailwaylinethatrejoicedorpalpitatedinthesome-
whatalarmingnamegorsafawddachaidraigodanheddogleddollônpen-
rhynareurdraethceredigionthereisareferencetodragonsteethamidthatjum-
blebuthedidntknowthatthentherewasnothingworthseeingtherebuthe-
lingeredanywaythewindwhippedhisfacedryingitslightlyanoldmanap-
pearedandsaidareyouhereforthenameithoughtasmuchitsalongonethats-
forsurebutihavesailedaroundtheworldandicanassureyouthatlongernam-
esexistelsewhereyoumustjourneyfartolocatethemdoyoubelievemeidosaid-
thorntonbecauseyoulookfamiliarnoidontneverthatthorntonbowedhis-
headherealisedthathisquestwasgoingtotakealotlongerthanhehadantici-
patedheheadedinasoutherlydirectionandeventuallywanderedintoapar-
tofwalessoremoteandgrimthateventhewelsharentawareofitnearthegro-
tesquevillageoflladlohchokedbytheundergrowthofthedenseforeststood-
theruinsofalongextinctcommunitythatwasonceamirrorimageofitsneigh-
bouraweirdreversalofthatfrightfulanomalybutthisdoesntmeanitwasap-
leasantplacethorntonwanderedamongtheshellsofoldbuildingstheyreal-
lydidlooklikeshellstoothoseofnightmarishgastropodsatlasthefoundthe-
signposthehadbeenlookingforitgavethenameofthevillageasyrotssihtrofyl-
laicepseputiedamiesuacebseirotsrehtoymfoynaniraeppalliwegallivsiht-
tahttbuodylsuoiresinowonderthecommunityimplodedwhilehewasmus-
ingthustherewasarustlegoodmorningimrussellsaidacreakingvoicethorn-
tonturnedandfoundhimselffacinganotheroldmanwhywasitalwaysold-
menwhomaterialisedtogivehimadvicebuthewaspoliteenoughandsaidhel-
lotoyoutheoldmanwavedagnarledhandyeshebeganmyformervillagedid-
haveamonstrouslyelongatednamebutthereareothersevenlongerelsewhere-
andbeyondthatiswhyimwavingthisgnarledhandatyouwheredidyoufindi-
taskedthorntontheoldmandroppedthegnarledhanditwashangingona-
treeidoenjoywavingitaboutnowandthenthankyouforsharingyourwis-
domsirandthorntonhastenedawayanddidntdarelookbackuntiltheforest-
wasfarbehindhimhekeptgoinguntilhefinallyreachedthecoastandinthe-
oldportoftenbyhewentaboardashipandsailedtodistantlandsalwaysseek-
ingthelongestplacenameinmassachusettshediscoveredalakecalledchargog-
gagoggmanchauuggagoggchaubunagungamauggbutnothinglongerthan-
thatintherestoftheamericancontinentandinnewzealandhevisitedtauma-
tawhakatangihangakoauauotamateaturipukakapikimaungahoronu-
kupokaiwhenuakitanatahuandcameawaybewilderedalwaysshewasmet-

44

byoldmenwithadviceatlastaftermanyyearsofwanderinghereturnedtoth-
esiteandthepeoplefromwhencehehadstartedoutitwastheclubhouseoftheel-
dritchexplorersclubtheyinterviewedhiminaroomthatwassphericaland-
hestoodatthebottomwherethesouthernpolemightbewhiletheyoccupieda-
balconysethighuponthenortherntropiclinedidyoufindthelongestplace-
nameofalltheyaskedthorntonexcelsiorlookedatthemandherecognisedthe-
facesofalltheoldmenwhohadapproachedhimtherewascaradocweaselica-
rusevansgammarayrusselltonguewagglechipchopjanuscronkorkward-
erunshackleernestonandothersididbetterthanthatthorntonsaiddefiantly-
whatdoyoumeantheycriedwhereveriwentidroppedaletterfrommypocket-
whenicrossedtheoceantheseletterssankontotheseabedbutalwaystheywere-
linkedtothelettersthatwentbeforeandallthosethatcameaftereventually-
thestringofletterscircledtheentireglobeandwhatofthathisinterrogatorsde-
mandedicreatedanewplaceintheprocessrepliedthorntonandcertainlyith-
asthelongestnameintheworlditssuchalongnamethatitencirclestheplane-
tandcomesbacktothebeginningagainindeeditformsaloopthatisinfinitewh-
enyousetoffforthatplacehowcanyoueverknowifyouhavereacheditsimulta-
neouslyyouwillbethereandnottherethatismyachievementjudgemeaccord-
inglytellusthenameofthisplacetheyinsistedareyousureyouwanttohearit-
theynoddedinassentsothorntontookadeepbreaththedeepestthathasever-
beentakenandspokethefollowingwordtheysenthimtoseekoutthelongestpla-
cenamintheworld...

"Enough! Please stop!" they pleaded.

But it was too late for that.

THE ESPLANADE

The exercise machines dominate the esplanade in the way that they do simply because they are always in use. People are constantly puffing and wheezing in the intimate embrace that signifies a passion for enhanced health and strength and the machines are never unwilling to be worked. Maintained by council lackeys, they are remarkably quiet despite the profusion of interlocking parts and the complexity of the gearing systems, which is just as well considering the fact they must operate throughout the night, in all weather. They hold an irresistible allure for the inhabitants of our coastal city.

The council grandees gave the exercise machines to us more than five years ago. They appeared from nowhere, unannounced, strange frameworks of aluminium and steel like avant-garde sculptures, and at first I assumed they were part of a misguided cultural project. But no, the true purpose was more realistic and sagacious. In an attempt to improve the wellbeing of the city, it had finally been decided that preventative health measures should be officially sanctioned, that the cult of fitness must be encouraged. And the initiative was a complete success, much to the astonishment of tubby sceptics.

Although at first it was considered somewhat daring to patronise such apparatus in full public view, for each machine required peculiar postures and contortions from the athlete, it took only a few days before the giggles of spectators were stifled and replaced with murmurs of appreciation and encouragement. A couple of weeks later, the spectators had vanished, disparaging their former passive roles and playing an active part in keeping the machines in motion. In short, everyone became a devotee, for the council had even provided devices suitable for the old, lame and sick as well as those with robust bodies.

Eventually the tubby sceptics embraced the fashion and soon they were less tubby and not sceptical at all. As for Leonora and myself: we had been among the first converts and it might be ventured without risk of censure for undue exaggeration that we rapidly became connoisseurs of the various contraptions on offer. Chiefly we favoured those special machines designed for couples, bizarre and almost insectile interweavings of tubes and shiny segments that positioned the man and woman in a selection of quasi-erotic situations.

The only inhabitants of the city who refrained from using the machines were the council grandees themselves, who remained bulkier and more awkward of movement than the population they managed. And yet they seemed happy enough when they appeared on the streets, as they did only infrequently, hurrying to conferences or formal dinners; but this happiness had none of the purity of true joy, the honest reaction to a positive improvement in one's life. Rather it seemed a simple relief, the lightness of soul that comes after a weighty responsibility or worry has been shrugged off. Consequently I felt an obscure pity for them.

But I was a fool back then and perhaps still am one. Leonora said to me one morning, "There is a secret to the exercise machines on the esplanade. I intend to find out what it is. Will you help me?"

"I don't see how we might achieve that," I replied.

"Come on, Thorny! Use your imagination for once. The council are up to something and doubtless the common men and women are the dupes. That's always the way it happens. It seems awfully important to the authorities that we work the machines, keep them going without a pause; and the expressions on the faces of the grandees are now those of debtors who suddenly no longer have to pay interest on their loans. Take it from me, somebody is *saving money*. And it's not us, that's for sure."

"Is that your best guess?" I asked her.

She nodded. I toyed with the notion that a bureaucratic swindle was in progress, that we had been ensnared by the machines, made slaves of the physical pleasure, only partly sexual in nature, they gave us in return for being manipulated. But the official reason for their existence, that they were there simply to improve our health, still seemed more plausible to me.

"Certainly there are savings when it comes to medical care," I pointed out, "for the population of the city is generally less prone to illness now. Obesity and its attendant problems have vanished almost completely…"

Leonora scowled at me. My naivety cracked under the harsh rays of her contempt and I almost saw the solid beams radiating from her eyes in devastating pulses. At once my objections collapsed into rubble.

47

"What do you suggest?" I murmured and she said:

"That's more like it! This is what I believe: the exercise machines are connected to hidden dynamos under the esplanade. When we operate the contraptions we turn the dynamos and generate electricity. The real power station has been turned off. We have been tricked into providing our own electrical energy. These devices aren't innocent at all. They are industrial treadmills!"

I pulled a face. "Can you prove those allegations?"

She reached out and used her thumbs and fingers to return my expression to its normal setting; and no matter how hard I struggled to grimace, her strength prevailed over mine. "Yes, we can prove them, I'm confident of that! But it will take a proper effort. We must call a strike! Somehow we must persuade people to stop using the machines. Then we'll see if the streetlamps come on at night and whether our television sets and electric kettles still work. You must think of a strategy, a way of returning the esplanade to its former tranquillity. That's your task, Thorny! You are a natural organiser…"

I wasn't and I'm still not. But I did what she asked.

Sabotage of the machines was the obvious solution but I couldn't damage the workings of all of them. Metal shields protected the internal mechanisms and an outraged citizen or law enforcement officer would apprehend me while I was bent over my task. It had to be faster than that, more unobtrusive. After a few nights of extremely restless sleep the answer came to me at breakfast while I was pouring olive oil over my toast…

Instead of impeding the movement of the cogs and axles, I made them turn more smoothly. The oil seeped through tiny holes in the outer shells and dripped onto the internal parts, reducing the friction by a considerable amount. It took only a few seconds to deal with each contraption in this manner and I wasn't even observed. Before long the first plaintive cry escaped from dismayed lips:

"This device has become too easy to operate! There simply isn't any resistance any more. I can't feel the benefit!"

Others agreed with this judgment. They dismounted.

It was night. The esplanade was quieter than it had ever been, for even the sea was utterly calm and nobody spoke. But the streetlamps still burned. Could it be the case that Leonora was wrong? The crescent moon gleamed but not like a sickle, for we had forgotten the use of such tools; indeed most of us had never known in the first place. The pause was pregnant and I was the father. I made no attempt to dissipate the tension: I had reverted into a pure spectator and even the act of shuffling my feet seemed too fantastic to contemplate. We waited and the minutes passed. Or did they? Nothing moved.

"Leonora!" I croaked helplessly.

A figure came running along the esplanade, a fat man who glowed with the effort of exertion like a sunset mounted on shoulders. His open jacket flapped with a horrible urgency, shiny black sails in a self-created storm, and his tie quested the air like a serpent or some other comparison rather more elaborate. He approached closer and I finally recognised him as Pompo Manners, mightiest of the council grandees. As he passed, he jabbed a powerful finger in my direction and swivelled his bulging bloodshot eyes with an audible grinding noise, corroded optical gyroscopes, until they were fastened on my guilty frame.

"Thornton Excelsior! This is entirely your fault. You fool…"

When we are moving normally and something happens to make us astonished, we often freeze. I was already frozen, so the shock of this utterance caused my muscles to loosen. I became fluid again and flowed faster than any oil into the prepared embrace of Leonora. How did Pompo Manners know I was to blame? How did he even know my name? Tremble in the shadow of the all-seeing council, my fellow citizens! From the safety of Leonora's arms I turned my head and called at the immensely broad back of the colossus:

"Yes sir! No sir! Forgive me. But for what?"

In truth we were all confused. Pompo reached the largest and most intricate of the machines, paused for a moment to catch a tiny percentage of his breath, no more than a token commission, and then inserted himself with difficulty into the web of steel. Perched uncomfortably on a narrow saddle he commenced pedalling with his feet and working levers with his arms. It was still night. The sea, clouds and stars had not moved at all. But the lamps burned, hissing in mild disapproval at our curiosity as we watched Pompo toil. His crimson cheeks turned orange, then yellow, then white and finally blue.

"He is overheating more than any man in history," Leonora remarked.

49

And still we watched without helping.

For a long time, perhaps hours, very little changed. The citizens stood and the council grandee jerked through his routine. Where were his colleagues? Snoring away the effects of large formal dinners, no doubt. Pompo maintained a steady rhythm and the stench of his sweat mingled with the smell of the paralysed sea, jellyfish, urchins and garlic. Then something happened. The sea quivered, the tide came in a fraction. Pompo increased his efforts, grimacing, determined to overcome the inertia of nature. A cloud dropped over the horizon with a clang. Then the reflected moonlight rippled. Pompo groaned an appeal:

"What's wrong with you? Won't you assist me?"

There was an embarrassed shuffling. Then someone stepped forward and mounted an adjacent machine and began pedalling too. The sea moved faster, more smoothly, lapped properly again. Other citizens capitulated and selected a device to operate. The stars grew dim. And with an awful grinding noise and a series of yelps that echoed off every building on the waterfront, the sun rose over the horizon like a damaged theatre prop. Wine light drenched our pallid faces and people laughed. And I was in disgrace for the remainder of my life and even in the most secure hiding place of all, the ultimate depths of Leonora's bosom, the insults still reached my ears.

THE ROTTEN OTTER

All irregularities will be handled by the forces controlling each dimension. Transuranic heavy elements may not be used where there is life. Medium atomic weights are available — Gold, Lead, Copper, Jet, Diamond, Radium, Sapphire, Silver, Steel, Wood, Cheese, Catnip, Drizzle, Rum, Gravy, Marmalade, Sea Foam, Hogwash and Bum Note. Hogwash and Bum Note have been assigned...

"What's that you're reading?" asked Bum Note.

"A message that just came through," said Hogwash, "on the astral aether. I wrote it down before I forgot the words. Like taking dictation from a god or the universe itself, it was. I'm flabbergasted."

"Hogwash!" exclaimed Bum Note.

"No it's not. It's perfectly sensible despite the fact it's a little abstruse. Some cosmic force has chosen us — you and me — to act as agents on some mission of unimaginable importance. It turns out that we aren't just simple explorers but elemental representatives of—"

Bum Note jumped up and down excitedly. "I wasn't passing judgment on any of that. I was merely calling your name aloud to alert you to the fact there's an otter with a blowpipe sitting on your bookshelf over there! You'd better duck your head before the dart that has been ejected from the weapon penetrates your exposed neck!"

"Ah yes. Thank you kindly, old chum. Whoosh."

"Why did you say 'whoosh'?" asked Bum Note. "Was it because the blowpipe dart couldn't be bothered to make that sound itself? You're too considerate, if you ask me. And why did you invite an otter assassin into your house anyway? That was rather unwise."

"I *didn't* invite him," insisted Hogwash from the floor.

Bum Note helped him up and they pondered together. The otter had vanished by this time but the dart was still quivering in the wall and smoke curled up from its point, proof that it had been coated with some corrosive poison. Hogwash licked his lips and said, "Maybe we ought to visit our wisest friend and get some advice."

"Good idea. But who exactly is our wisest friend?"

"Thornton Excelsior, I suppose..."

And so they came to see me. As a tack of all jades I'm pretty good at solving the problems of fictional characters. Just don't come to me if you are real, which I feel confident is your own present condition. I was sitting in the bathtub reading a first edition copy of *Gentlemen Prefer Aardvarks* by Anteater Loos when the doorbell rang. I jumped up and dripped nudely to the front door to berate it.

"Use the knocker next time!" I shouted at the doorbell.

Then I saw Hogwash and Bum Note.

What a coincidence that they turned up just as I was forced to answer the door! It saved me two trips from the bath and I was grateful for that. I welcomed them into my house and listened to what they had to say. Then I read the message that Hogwash had received over the astral aether and I twisted my face in response to the scientific inaccuracy of it, but it was my duty to assist them in any way I could, so I said:

"I'm familiar with the exploits of this otter. He's a transdimensional being known as Tarka the Rotter. He clearly plans to take over this universe and considers you to be a threat to his scheme. You are, after all, official agents of the Cosmic Mind. This message is proof of that. Tarka tried to launch a pre-emptive strike against you and he'll surely try again."

"What should we do?" gasped Hogwash.

"Pre-empt his next pre-emption. Find a way of beating him at his own game. And I'm not referring to chess or mah jong but assassination! You are explorers. That is your function in life: you explore. There must be a remote land somewhere, unknown to all of us, where the largest blowpipe in creation can be found. It simply stands to reason. Find that land and fetch that blowpipe and stealthily substitute it for the one Tarka presently employs and you can be assured of defeating his rotten schemes."

Those were my words and they had the desired impact…

Off hurried Hogwash and Bum Note to brand new regions. They scaled the Mountains of Brrrr, trudged the Deserts of Sighh and Waded the Bogs of Flussh, entering previously unexplored territory in the same way that a pair of trousers might enter an incorrectly constructed analogy. I waited for them to return with a blowpipe so long that it stretched all the way around the world or else with a blowpipe that flared so widely it was just like the dome of the sky. In the first instance, after the substitution was made, Tarka would puff the poisoned dart into his own back; in the second, a hurricane would form in the mouth of the weapon and reverse the direction of the dart, lodging it fatally in that horrid Rotter's throat.

Such was my expectation; but I had neglected to take the daftness of the explorers into account. When they did finally arrive at my door again, I was situated in the bathtub reading Anteater Loos' long-awaited sequel, *But Gentlemen Mount Pangolins,* and when I jumped out and nakedly invited them inside, they had a tale to tell that confounded me to no small degree, to approximately 270° if truth be stated.

In the incense-wreathed, sitar-saturated community of Lentilville, they had obtained the biggest blowpipe of all, just as I'd suggested, but in that tie-dyed place, with its little bells and organic wholefoods and meditation classes, the word 'blow' had a specific and unusual meaning. It was slang for hashish, man. That's cannabis resin to you and me, brother. And a vast rock of the potent black stuff was included in the bowl of that pipe, the pipe they had bought and conveyed home.

"And where is that incorrect pipe now?" I demanded.

"We already made the switch," explained Bum Note, "and Tarka didn't even notice until it was too late. We struck a light for him and the heady smoke went deep into his otterly lungs and he mellowed out considerably, so much in fact that he no longer wants to take over our universe. So the danger has been neutralised and we've won! But the fumes are harsh on his throat and he says he wants a name change from Tarka the Rotter to Tarka the Cougher. Is that acceptable to the Cosmic Mind?"

I shrugged my shoulders and claimed not to know the answer. But after they departed, I stood in front of the mirror and tugged off my mask and laughed heartily. For I'm not really Thornton Excelsior. Just like them I'm an agent, a medium atomic weight, but neater.

Behold! I am Catnip!

THE DUCKS OF HAZARD

Professor Vokisrep has done it again: for the second time in just one year he has successfully failed to destroy the world. What a marvel of twisted science that fellow is! First he invented a chemical intended to give amphibians enormous fiscal aptitude. He empted flasks of this noxious stuff into sluggish rivers that drained into marshes and he waited for the transformed newts and frogs to rise out of their weedy ponds and invade the stock exchanges of the great European capitals. But they never emerged to play the markets and precipitate a fiendish global recession. The rivers were already so polluted by the waste products of human industry that the professor's secret chemical was neutralised, adulterated or diluted before it even reached its target consumers.

So then he returned to the laboratory and decided to try a different approach. This time, after tinkering quite a lot with thermionic valves and variable resistors, he managed to create a machine that projected weird rays at boxes of eggs arranged on his workbench. The idea was to stimulate the growth of the ovoids so that they hatched into veritable monsters that would rampage around the continents: the eggs were those of crocodiles, snakes, ostriches and various lizards. But there was a mix-up with the batch delivered to him and Professor Vokisrep unwittingly subjected ordinary duck eggs to the fateful purple beams. They hatched and the ducklings grew so rapidly that they burst the laboratory apart before he could switch off the machine. Then they quacked him to death.

Those giant waterfowl wandered the landscape in the vicinity of the ruined laboratory for several days, looking for a pond large enough to accommodate them, and eventually they ended up on the platform of the nearest village railway station. A locomotive had just pulled in and the birds perched on the carriages for a rest, one per roof, and that's where they remained when the train chuffed off. The ultimate destination was Chester but the feathered hoboes never got that far: when crossing the Malvern range the gradient was too steep with all the extra weight, so the driver put the brakes on and scattered his unwanted passengers by jabbing at them with three brooms lashed together. Away they flapped and landed in the garden of Thornton Excelsior, who happens to be me. I decided to take retaliatory measures at once.

I reached for the telephone and rang Hogwash and Bum Note and invited them to stay for the weekend. They accepted with gratitude. Then I hid in my garden shed and watched proceedings through a spy hole. The two explorers arrived on a motorcycle with a sidecar and because this tale seems to be set in an anachronistic travesty of the real world they wore goggles instead of modern helmets with visors and they sported large wax moustaches. They also said, "What ho?" a lot but it was a question I was unable to answer because I didn't actually know what *ho* it was. And even if I had known I wouldn't have revealed my place of concealment by shouting out the answer. They didn't see the mutated mallards until the engine of the motorcycle had been turned off and it was too late to escape. And so…

"Duck!" bellowed Bum Note.

Hogwash threw himself to the ground, bashing his nose on a stone, before realising his mistake. "Ah, you weren't asking me to take evasive action but merely describing the creature yonder."

He clambered to his feet painfully and Bum Note cried, "Duck!"

"Yes, I can see there's more than one of—"

A massive yellow beak attached to an immense head pecked down with enormous force onto the crown of Hogwash's head, and the impact knocked him to the ground again, where he clobbered his chin, and the exposure to all those hefty superlatives probably didn't help.

"That time I was giving you a command," said Bum Note.

"Humph!" Hogwash huffed unhappily.

The first duck closed in to renew its attack and the others also waddled gigantically into the fray. Bum Note squeaked, "How shall we defeat them?" and Hogwash considered the problem and replied:

"If we allow them to eat us we can get stuck in their throats and then they will surely choke to death; but even if they succeed in swallowing us we may still be in a position to give them a fatal bout of indigestion. That's my best plan under the present circumstances."

And I rubbed my hands in glee as I watched from the shed.

The hazardous ducks, courtesy of Professor Vokisrep, loomed above the pair of hapless explorers, beaks unsheathed for the coming massacre. Hogwash and Bum Note trembled like scared men, which is a dreadfully bad simile because that's what they already were, and they held hands and closed their eyes, waiting for the end to begin with the next big peck.

But something unexpected happened and I groaned in frustration because it seems to be the most predictable fact of my entire life that unexpected things suddenly occur to upset my schemes. Without exchanging an intelligible word between them, the ducks lifted ponderously into the sky, summoned by a desire greater than the urge to duckimate — I mean decimate — with murderous beak work the daffy duo. Ah well!

I had no choice but to emerge from the shed and greet my visitors as if I was delighted to see them, feigning ignorance of the foul anecdote they had been in and making dramatic faces when they told me about the seriousness of the incident. And so the weekend passed…

A week or so later, I was sitting in my office in the Eldritch Explorers' Club when there was a knock on the door and Hogwash and Bum Note entered and said, "We have worked out why the ducks flew away just like that. It was the one inexplicable part of the adventure but we've cracked it now. The migratory instinct! That's what seized hold of them at the crucial moment and it was too powerful to resist. But we have no idea where they've gone."

"South," I answered promptly. "That's the natural law."

"But where is south?" they asked.

I reached for an atlas and looked up that destination in an index and then I checked the grid references on one of the maps. I frowned and consulted a larger scale map of the same region, and then one still larger, and so on, zooming in on a worrying fact. At last I announced:

"It seems to be the case, gentlemen, that the precise location of 'south' is this very room in this very building in this very town in this very province in this very country."

"How very inconvenient," they said.

I glanced up. The first duck crashed through the window and killed all three of us. And that's how we died yet again.

KNIGHT ON A BEAR MOUNTAIN

Thornton Excelsior was staying at an inn called The Tall Story and in the evenings he would come down into the taproom and drink a pint of ale in the corner opposite the fire. It took several visits before he realised that it wasn't logs or coals that were burning on the hearth but the unpublished manuscripts of unsuccessful writers.

He learned this one evening when a page came loose and spilled onto the flagstones. Before it charred to ash, Thornton managed to read a few sentences and then he knew it was a novel that was blazing away. When he went to the bar to order another ale, he decided to broach the subject with the innkeeper, who served him.

"Do you always use literary works for fuel?"

"These days, yes," came the reply.

"Isn't that rather wasteful?"

"Nothing to do with me," replied the innkeeper, a burly fellow by the name of Hywel. "It wasn't my idea, but this inn is frequented by creative types and some of them are authors and they often grow dissatisfied with the stories they are writing and decide to burn them here. I don't forbid it because it saves me fetching firewood."

"A page fell out just now. Does that often happen?"

Hywel nodded. "Most evenings."

"So some pages survive intact?" Thornton persisted.

Hywel rubbed his chin. "Rarely do complete pages emerge unscathed, but many isolated words and phrases escape being burned, yes. Instead of throwing them back on, I keep them."

And he reached down somewhere behind the bar and lifted up a bulky box full of disjointed sentences.

"That's amazing," said Thornton.

"Reach in and take a handful, if you like," replied Hywel, shaking the box, making the charred words dance.

"Why should I do that?" wondered Thornton.

"It's good for the soul, I don't know why. Here, take the entire box and play with the contents for a while."

There was something quaint and amusing in the absurd suggestion and so that's what Thornton did. He went back to his table and dipped into the box and began moving the words around, as if he was kneading dough. It brought a smile to his face, strangely.

I happened to be watching from my own corner.

Gazing at Thornton I couldn't work out the reason why he was here. It wasn't just that he was lonely in the way that any traveller gets lonely, but there was something deeper going on.

Perhaps he was hoping to find a sweetheart, a girl in a million, and it's not such a bad place for that. And yet it occurred to me that with a global population of seven billion, there must be 7000 girls in a million running around at random and if they decided to enter The Tall Story at the same time, Thornton would die of admiration and suffocation. Which reminds me: the ventilation was playing up.

There's a big grille set into one of the walls and a fan that sucks out the fetid air and cigar smoke and the musical notes of the regulars. This grille strongly resembles an ancient knight's helmet, with a visor. And I believe Thornton thought so too, though I can't say why I'm so sure. As I watched him churning the words, I called to him:

"Why not use them to make a brand new story?"

He looked up at me sharply, but there was no anger in his expression. I probably had just vocalised his intentions. He said, "Do you really think that would be a wise thing to do?"

"Nothing is wise in The Tall Story, my friend."

He smiled and I winked back.

So he pulled out fistfuls of loose words and let them fall onto the table and it took very little rearrangement before a coherent narrative appeared and I knew this from his astonishment.

"I can't see it from here," I cried. "Read it out aloud."

"Yes, do that," agreed Hywel.

So Thornton cleared his throat and said, "It seems to be about a knight and a bear. The knight is Sir Jasper."

"Go right ahead," we urged and so he did:

"There was once a knight called Sir Jasper who rode through the land and back again with a female squire…"

I closed my eyes and I pictured it perfectly.

58

Across many different landscapes they went and Sir Jasper hadn't taken off his armour for weeks because he thought it would be a shame not to have an adventure in it first. At bedtime he made a cold companion for Sue, who always slept naked, but even a cold companion is better than none at all in the unknown wilderness.

Sir Jasper treated his squire with tenderness and passion; and he would caress Sue in the mornings, as the lazy smoke of the previous night's fire drifted across the campsite. At first Sue shivered at the touch of the iron gauntlet between her soft legs, but Sir Jasper treated her gently despite his passion and Sue nearly always came strongly with the sensation that she was releasing all her fear and tension.

She wished for more than this, she desperately wanted to give pleasure in return, but Sir Jasper had made a vow. Until he had an adventure in his armour and could take it off with a clear conscience, he wouldn't be in a practical position to enjoy Sue properly. They did try to, once, but it was so uncomfortable that it just didn't work.

"An adventure worthy of a brave knight first!" he said.

They rode through forests of myrtle and cedar, past the stubs of ruined castles, along the shorelines of brooding lakes. These regions were mostly depopulated, lonely, isolated and sombre.

Eventually they came to a flat country on the edge of a stagnant sea. It was all marsh and swamp, with complicated routes winding between the lagoons and quicksands, and wills-o'-the-wisp at dusk to entice them off the path. It was a curiously languid land, a drain on the soul. In the day, willpower was strangely lacking, but mosquitoes and dogged persistence urged them on. Catfish too, which leapt out of the pools to bite their laps. Sir Jasper and Sue were grateful to arrive at a settlement. It was a town in which every building was a windmill.

It was late in the afternoon and the sun was low.

"Let's look for accommodation here," suggested Sir Jasper, as he rode carefully between the swishing sails.

The local chief was Pungent Hugh, miller of millers, grinder of black bog-rush and pumper of bilge, who protected his people with dykes and towels. He welcomed the knight and his squire with a handshake and a meal at a table in the kitchen of his own house. The bread was awful. Then when Sir Jasper had finished belching through his visor, Pungent Hugh made a little speech. He said:

"How grateful I am to meet such a noble hero."

"And why is that?" asked Sir Jasper, with much interest and not a little suspicion. "Dragons in this territory?"

"No, those creatures are mostly mythological, I'm afraid. But we do need protection from a ferocious talking bear that roams these parts and raids our town at night. He doesn't come every night but always when we least expect him. He smashes the sails of our windmills with his paws or spins them backwards until they break."

"A talking bear?" blinked Sir Jasper. "In a swamp! Are you sure?" He turned to Sue with a sceptical shrug.

Pungent Hugh wasn't dismayed by his reaction. "Absolutely certain. I have heard it with my own ears. Oh, I know what you're thinking: bears normally live in the mountains, don't they? Maybe this one does too, but he comes down to visit us after sunset."

"I accept the quest! I shall sally forth to slay the creature!"

Pungent Hugh bowed. "Thank you."

"I'll start tomorrow morning," said Sir Jasper.

Pungent Hugh offered the pair a comfortable room for the night with a real straw bed. The sun went down and bled on the lagoons; it was lovely beyond words and yet worrying, and the knight and his squire lingered at the window for only a few minutes before turning away from the sight. In the dusk they felt suddenly very weary.

"Perhaps the bear will come tonight," said Sue.

"That's feasible," agreed Sir Jasper.

They went to bed, but the knight remained awake as long as he could, his ears straining to hear any unnatural noise outside, but the swishing of the windmills was constant, rhythmic and lulled him to sleep against his will. When he awoke, the sky through the window was pale and big birds with extremely long legs were flying somewhere. He looked down at the marsh and inhaled the astringent fumes.

"Shall I fetch your horse?" asked Sue sleepily.

"No." Sir Jasper buckled on his sword. "I'll do it myself. I want you to remain here. I have a premonition…"

"You can't seek the talking bear by yourself."

"I can and I will, my dear girl."

"But I pledged to serve you always!" objected Sue.

"That's correct," said the knight, "and so now I expect you to serve me in this matter too. Stay here. Await my return. I have a feeling that if we go together something bad will happen."

Sue sat up in bed, straw sticking to her face. "Did you have a dream, is that what happened? Tell me, please."

Sir Jasper turned to look down at his faithful squire.

"Nothing like that. Just a hunch."

He refused to debate the subject further. They went down and met the miller in the kitchen and he prepared breakfast for them. Then Sir Jasper bade them farewell and went outside.

And off he galloped again, glad to be fulfilling his chivalrous role at last. It dimly occurred to him that he didn't really need to go off and seek the bear; he could simply remain in the town until the bear decided to pay another visit, but there was something unheroic about not taking an active part in looking for danger. What genuine knight ever sits still and allows monsters or villains to come to him?

The traditions must be followed scrupulously. Besides, he didn't like the town. So he kept going, looking for the beast, even though he hadn't been given a full description. What if he challenged an innocent bear by mistake? That never occurred to him.

As the sun crept up the sky, it grew hotter and hotter and the marsh and lagoons became shimmering mirrors of quicksilver. Sir Jasper began to sweat profusely inside his armour. He was grateful for all the holes in his visor that let the air in. The sky was cloudless, but swarms of biting insects cast a little filigreed shade. He kept going and stopped only once for lunch. The day passed very slowly.

At last the strength of the bloated sun weakened.

Sir Jasper cooled in his armour…

He knew where he was headed thanks to an eccentric line of reasoning he had decided to pursue. Due north! For when the evening finally came and the stars appeared, the constellation of Ursa Major would be directly ahead, frosty and bright. His destination.

A constellation makes a poor roof for a man, but not for a bear. And what other roof would a talking bear choose to dwell under? Ursa Major is the Great Bear, and a real bear that can articulate meaningful sentences must surely be the greatest of its kind.

Sir Jasper peered anxiously into the far distance, but still no mountains loomed. The land remained flat. The sun sank into a lagoon and the foam on his horse's mouth turned pink. Still there were no peaks visible on the horizon. Twilight was followed by dusk; the smell of decaying vegetation gave way to that of smoke. A volcano?

No, it was a campfire, and the bear sat warming its paws in front of it. A pot of stereotypical porridge bubbled on the embers. Sir Jasper found it impossible to urge his steed forward, so he softly dismounted and creaked stealthily towards his foe. Ursa Major did indeed twinkle, above him and also on his armour. He grimaced inside his helmet as the bear turned its large head at his approach, but realising that his expressions of fear were hidden, the knight drew his long sword from its scabbard with a confident flourish and ran forward on stiff legs.

The bear stood up. It fixed the charging knight with its wild eyes and demanded, "Who the bloody hell are you?"

Sir Jasper had known it was going to be a talking bear, but actually hearing the words emanating from that mighty jaw was an experience he wasn't really prepared for. He went numb. The sword slipped from his fist. This was precisely the reaction the bear was hoping for. The tactic rarely failed. It opened its arms to receive its visitor, which it intended to crush inside the iron shell, rather than wasting time trying to get him out first. It's always nice to be economical.

The plan almost worked, but Sir Jasper had a secret.

Before he had become a knight, he had wanted to be an actor. He wasn't very good at it (critics said he was too wooden) but he'd gained some knowledge of the mechanical tricks used by theatre companies to increase the astonishment factor of a production. The most obvious and simple of these devices was the pantomime horse. Worked by levers and springs on the inside, a single man could operate the mock creature with amazing efficiency and lifelike dexterity.

Something in the bear's tone made Sir Jasper wonder if a similar trick was being played here. Instead of trying to slow his headlong rush, he accelerated and jumped. The bear closed its paws around nothing. The knight came down on the bear, straddling its shoulders. Sure enough there was a row of buttons running all the way down the beast's back. What's more, they looked ready to pop. Sir Jasper reached over and undid the top one. It was just enough.

The costume burst.

Unfortunately for him, there wasn't a man inside, as he'd hoped. Sir Jasper had assumed that bigger things hold smaller things, not the other way around. The new being that stood among the tattered remains of the artificial bear was — a hippopotamus!

It rolled its eyes and lisped, "Thank goodness for that! It was such a tight fit in there!" But Sir Jasper wasn't deceived. He looked for the row of buttons, found them and undid the top one of this costume too, and the hippo burst to reveal an elephant, which reared high and trumpeted, "A blessed relief to be out of that, what?"

Yet Sir Jasper still didn't relax. How could he?

Another undoing of a button, another fabric detonation and now the knight was confronted by a blue whale. Before it could utter a word, he fumbled for the next button. Now he was in the branches of a gigantic redwood tree. He felt dizzy. He screamed as he undid this final button, for what burst out of the tree was something he had suspected was the real villain all along, though he hadn't acknowledged the fact to himself...

It was an impossibly high mountain. Its lower slopes were covered in snow and dead climbers. Sir Jasper clung tightly to the summit, but as the peak rose into the sky and beyond the atmosphere, he came to regret the holes in his visor that let the air out...

The box of words and phrases was empty, so Thornton sighed and turned his attention to his ale. Hywel frowned.

"That's an abrupt ending to the story! What a shame!"

"No, I think it's the only ending that fits properly," said Thornton. But it was clear he felt cheated by himself.

"It makes plenty of sense to me," I added.

Thornton glanced up, saw my expression. "You took it to heart, didn't you? What do you really think of it?"

"Disjointed. I'm not blaming you for that, of course. You only had a limited selection of previously used words to work with. But it provided an answer to something I have been wondering about for a long time. I knew Sir Jasper personally, you see."

"How is that possible? It was just a random story."

"Coincidence, I guess," I said.

We said nothing more for five minutes; then Thornton picked up his ale and came over to sit at my table. He sat next to me and we clinked glasses and he leaned close. "Sue?"

I nodded. "I remained in the town of windmills for a week. When it was clear that Sir Jasper wasn't coming back, I left and headed home. It wasn't possible to remain there longer; Pungent Hugh began to make it plain I had overstayed my welcome."

"And you eventually found yourself in The Tall Story?"

"Yes and that's where I still am."

I was about to say more, when the front door crashed open and a huge figure muffled in a long cloak entered the inn. It carried a thick bundle of loose papers under one brawny arm. Thornton jerked in alarm, but neither Hywel nor myself were unduly scared.

"Another one?" called the innkeeper jocularly.

"Afraid so," came the gruff reply. "I just can't get the characterization right. And the tone seems all wrong."

"Back to the beginning," commented Hywel.

The newcomer nodded and flung the manuscript onto the fire. Then it turned to leave, but as it did so, the loose hem of its cloak caught around a table leg and pulled free. For a moment I found myself staring at a bear. Then it snatched up the cloak, rolled it into a ball and flung that on top of the burning novel, laughing as it did so.

The door slammed again and I pressed my face to the narrow window in time to see the lumbering shape being swallowed by a freak summer snowstorm that conveniently appeared to cover its tracks. I glanced at the fire, knowing that some of the words would probably survive and might even help to tell a sequel to this very tale.

THE CHEEKY MONKEY

If like repels like and opposites attract, how is it possible that Hogwash and Bum Note, two of the cheekiest and hairiest personalities on the planet, made the acquaintance of The Cheeky Monkey one evening in a grove of tamarind trees somewhere in the depths of Bananaskindia? Maybe because they aren't magnets, not yet at any rate. That's my best guess.

I'm not a magnet either, but I am almost a magnate because I recently invested heavily in a déjà vu plantation, growing some of the most poignant déjà vus this side of the past, and the returns have been enormous. The returns have been enormous. Did I just say that? People told me there was no future in the déjà vu business but they were doubly, even triply wrong.

The returns have been enormous. Now where was I?

Here, of course, where else? My name is Thornton Excelsior and I take a keen interest in the comings and goings of Hogwash and Bum Note, the daftest explorers in the annals of daftness, and in the canals too whenever those are available. On behalf of the Eldritch Explorers' Club, of which I am currently stoolman, our chairs having collapsed thanks to woodworm and obesity, I dispatched them to Bananaskindia to map that slippery land.

A keen interest in their comings and goings… Am I repeating myself?

Especially in the goings. They are a liability.

Bananaskindia is a fruitful region of the world and yet it is rife with hazards, including the dreaded Recycling Cyclones, a meteorological phenomenon found nowhere else, partly because nobody has bothered to look in any other location and partly because local storms don't have the necessary paperwork to cross the Bananaskindian border. Let's be grateful!

When you are exposed to a Recyclone, as they are known for short, all the molecules in your body are rearranged and you become something new and generally much more useless than before; the ghost of a spirit level, perhaps, or a pocket knife so sharp it cuts through any pocket it is dropped into. Those are just a couple of examples taken at random from my brain. I wanted Hogwash and

Bum Note to be overwhelmed and transformed like that. If I can't get rid of them properly, at least I can get them altered.

Or so I reasoned. But my wishes were thwarted.

And it was The Cheeky Monkey's fault…

To reach Bananaskindia, Hogwash and Bum Note trekked through the purple passes of Neplum and descended into the plains and ready salteds of the frontier region. On the border sat a wise man, a sage, who blinked at them with his third eye and said, "If you want my advice, you should always turn the other cheek. Go in peace, my friends."

"We'll remember your words," answered the explorers.

They proceeded south, reaching the city of Delhicatessen a few weeks later, where they stocked up on provisions before resuming their journey. It was hot and they sweated under the sun like punctured barrels; too hot even for a better simile than that. How delighted they were to each the cool shade of the sweet tamarind forest!

In a small clearing not long after sunset, they encountered The Cheeky Monkey, who lay full length on the ground, weeping thick tears and clenching and unclenching his poor little hands in adjectival dismay.

"Look at his poor little hands!" cried Hogwash.

"They certainly don't have a bank balance or possession of properties, land and other assets, if that's what you mean," returned Bum Note.

"Shall we enquire the cause of his grief?"

"Yes. Why do you sob like that, O prostrate primate?"

"It's because… because… because I am so very ugly. That's why! All my life I have been mocked because of my cheeks. I have too many of them on my face and in fact they grow on the other side of my head too. They go right round and join up again in a loop…"

"Encircled by cheeks! A wheel of cheeks!" marvelled Hogwash.

"And the other animals make fun?"

"Almost every day," sniffed The Cheeky Monkey.

Hogwash and Bum Note conferred together briefly and then they comforted the supine creature with the wise words the sage had given them: "Turn the other cheek. That's all you have to do when insults are hurled at you. Simply turn the other cheek. It's easy enough."

The Cheeky Monkey digested this advice. "Very well, I shall!" And that's exactly what happened.

Maybe he thought he needed the practise, or perhaps he felt offended by the mere presence of the two explorers, but whatever the reason it can't be denied that the outcome was unexpected and astounding, although perfectly logical in its own way. The monkey began rolling.

The problem was that he simply had too many cheeks to make turning the other one a safe procedure. And Hogwash and Bum Note had neglected to inform him *when* to stop turning them. The Cheeky Monkey therefore accelerated along the ground like a horizontal tornado.

"I always knew I'd go far!" he called back dizzily.

Hogwash and Bum Note watched him rotate. To my eternal chagrin, this was the moment that a Recyclone decided to form with the intention of spinning the explorers into a transformational oblivion; it grew directly in the path of The Cheeky Monkey and there was a collision of vortices.

What happened next? No one is sure. The axis of the Recyclone was perpendicular to that of The Cheeky Monkey and my mathematical abilities aren't sophisticated enough to work out which helix dominated the other. Maybe they combined forces or cancelled each other out. I fear it was the latter option. Certainly it is the case that my schemes were foiled yet again. Unless…

There is always the possibility that Hogwash was transformed, molecule by molecule, into Bum Note, and vice versa. That's exactly the sort of thing that would happen to them. So I'm going back to my déjà vu plantation. Again.

THE MELODY TREE

Everybody knows that Hogwash earned his name when he went into the wrong sauna during an expedition to Gruntland and fell into the plunge pool while it was full of the pigs that governed the country; but the reason for Bum Note's cognomen has been a mystery until now. The truth is that he got stuck in the branches of a melody tree and by the time his ordeal was over his buttock cheeks were very sore. A melody tree's bark is worse than its height, that's why, and the roughness chafed his essentials while he awaited rescue.

Now permit me to outline the reasons for his foolish decision to climb the melody tree in the first place: he wanted to pluck a notefruit. It seems that Bum Note was tone deaf and thought that ingesting the fruit would give him the appreciation of music that his own genetic heritage hadn't bothered to. Somehow he persuaded Hogwash to accompany him, despite the immense dangers involved in making the journey, for the nearest melody tree grows on the distant island of Opus, and a wall of mountains surrounds that stronghold.

They appealed to me for funding but I didn't give it to them, mainly because I'm not Thornton Excelsior and I don't have access to the coffers of the Eldritch Explorers' Club; Thornton is taking a short break to do some exploring of his own and he has left me in charge of this tale. My name is Jorge I. Barra and I'm a Texican, half Texan, half Mexican, half vulgar fraction, half polite fraction, a double man in total, twice as grand as any normal fellow. Being a Texican is something I would recommend if I could.

But I can't, because I'm the only true one destined to exist.

Anyway, to resume my narrative, the voyage to Opus was a risky one and the canoe that Hogwash and Bum Note chartered was carved from a gigantic banana; they borrowed it from the museum of the Eldritch Explorers' Club and because Thornton was away they sneaked it out unopposed. Even though I was left in charge I lacked the authority to molest them because I'm not a full member. I might be a Texican but I Texican't do everything, that goes without saying; too bad I just said it.

The banana canoe formerly belonged to Zumboo, the monkey god, and so it was watertight and unlikely to capsize.

And yet the journey between, over and through the mighty waves of the stormy ocean was dreadful enough to make me feel seasick as I write these words, or possibly my nausea stems from the fact that I'm bouncing on a trampoline; for some reason Thornton's office here in the clubhouse contains no other item of furniture, and because the trampoline in question is exactly the same size as the room that contains it, I have no choice but to stand on it. Every rumble of a truck in the street outside, every earthquake in a distant land, causes the thing to vibrate and these vibrations gradually build up into a powerful oscillation and there's nothing I can do but go along with it.

Yes, my name is Jorge I. Barra and I have my ups and downs...

People sometimes ask me what the 'I' stands for. It stands for me, of course! What does *your* 'I' stand for? But to return to my tale, Hogwash and Bum Note finally reached the imposing shores of Opus Isle and they circumnavigated it with deft paddlestrokes; yet the cliffs were sheer, smooth and slippery with green slime. There was no way to climb them.

"Look!" cried Hogwash. "A door. I wonder if it's unlocked?"

It wasn't, but Bum Note had a key.

"Do you really? Will it fit?" asked Hogwash doubtfully.

"Yes. It's the only key suitable for any lock on this island. It's the key of G# Minor, a key rarely employed in orchestral works, though I believe Scriabin was one significant composer who proved an exception to that rule. The problem is that I'm tone deaf and so—"

"Don't worry. I'll do the whistling!" cried Hogwash.

And he did; and the door unlocked itself and swung open, and so they were able to paddle their canoe into the gap thus revealed, passing through the mountains with ease. Along a narrow channel they went, right into the calm and verdant heart of Opus, and directly before them stood a melody tree laden with notefruit. Bum Note jumped for joy.

"Sit down, you'll capsize us!" warned Hogwash.

"No I won't, for this is the banana canoe of Zumboo; and we have to stand to get out of it anyway. Up you get!"

They moored the vessel to the bank and skipped lightly o'er the pasturage, a gentle breeze ruffling their fictional hair.

69

"Help me climb onto the twisted trunk and then I'll pull you up after me," said Bum Note as he reached the base of the magnificent melody tree. A rich copper colour it was, with dark green leaves clumped together like a conductor's spare fist; the notefruits resembled crotchets, minims and semi-quavers. As the two explorers began climbing the trunk, a heavy cloud passed overhead and enormous raindrops started to fall.

"That cloud looks ready to burst on us," observed Hogwash.

"There's a notefruit almost within reach. I'll pluck it and eat it and then we can descend and look for proper shelter; the canopy of this tree won't be sufficient to prevent us getting drenched."

"Maybe we can invert the canoe and use it as a roof?"

"But it's a giant banana. People would gossip!"

"They never need to find out…"

Poor Hogwash had forgotten that their adventures always get written up by some member of the Eldritch Explorers' Club. Too bad. But he's not wholly stupid, a fact demonstrated by his next comment, which he made while blinking furiously through the increasing rain at Bum Note above him. "How can you be *certain* that the eating of a notefruit will give you increased musical ability? It might turn you into a note instead…"

"Only if I swallow the seeds inside," said Bum Note, as he plucked the nearest fruit, which happened to be a quaver, from its stalk, and crammed it into his mouth. "Gobble, munch, yum. Urgh!"

"What's wrong? Did you swallow the seeds?"

Bum Note nodded; then the downpour began and it slicked the trunk of the melody tree and made it too slippery for safe descent. The two explorers were forced to sit on a branch and endure the diabolical deluge until it seemed likely that the drops of rain would actually kill them. What creature has too many paws, each one of which is too big for its body? A man riddled with rain! But the riddle only works if the word 'paws' is spelled 'pores'.

"I can feel the seeds growing inside me. I'm about to turn into a note. This is good news: after the transformation you can take shelter inside me and protect yourself from pluvial perforation."

"Take shelter inside you? What note are you likely to become?"

"One with a roof and rooms. A♭."

There was a long pause…

"I don't get it," said a voice. It belonged to Thornton Excelsior and it issued from his massive mouth; he was still far away on his own expedition but he had leaned across the margins to poke his head into this tale. Entering the prose sideways, the perspective was all wrong and the head nearly filled the office where I was bouncing on the trampoline, forcing me to throw myself down to avoid being crushed by his expressions.

"You don't get it? A*b* is a synonym for an apartment."

"Silly me," he said slowly.

THE REVERSED COMMA

The ordinary comma creates pauses in text; it logically follows that the reversed comma gives prose a push, accelerating it sometimes beyond the point of breathlessness into a blur or scream. A box of these extremely rare punctuation marks turned up inside a volume on the laws of motion: the pages of that thick tome had been cut away to make a secret hollow space sufficiently large to securely hold the box.

Thornton Excelsior does not remember how the book and thus the box came into his possession. But we know that he once sprinkled a handful of reversed commas into a yellowing copy of the *Highway Code*: the text immediately broke its own laws by exceeding the mandatory speed limit in an urban zone. Reversed commas are more properly known as *ammocs*, hence the phrase "to run ammoc".

Serious attempts to create interstellar engines by composing entire novels exclusively with reversed commas are destined to fail: nothing can exceed the speed of light entertainment.

BLACK OPS

When he reached the reception desk, Thornton Excelsior said, "I've come about the vacancy advertised in the newspaper. I have experience in all the necessary areas and I—"

The receptionist pointed at a door. "Go through there. Dr Vaughan and Dr Frazer require you immediately."

Thornton paused. "Don't I get an interview? Don't I even need to fill out an application form for the job?"

The receptionist shook her head emphatically. This struck him as odd, but he reminded himself that the position was in *Black Ops*, so irregular procedures were probably normal. Perhaps they were testing him in some obscure fashion? He went through the door and found himself in gloom. A voice from nowhere said, "Are you new?"

Thornton stuttered, "Yes, I saw the advert in the paper and—"

"You start at once! Get ready!"

Another voice, equally bodiless snapped, "Scalpel!"

Thornton dared not move a muscle.

The first voice cried, "What are you waiting for? Pass him the scalpel! Hurry man, we don't have all day!"

Thornton lurched forward and tripped over something. He got slowly to his feet, steadying himself by resting his hands on a low table just in front of him. Something soft and wet lay there. His fingers felt sticky now. He groped around with them and felt a sharp pain along the back of his hand. The second voice barked in his ear:

"What are you doing? You're not operating on yourself!"

"Clamps!" screamed the first voice.

"Tie off that vein there, you oaf!" growled the first.

Thornton retreated, knocked the back of his head on a machine that started emitting a series of frantic beeps. He gasped, "I have experience in the relevant areas! I know all about sabotage, propaganda, disorientation! I can manipulate foreign media—"

The owner of the first invisible voice made no attempt to conceal his contempt. "This is a circumcision!"

"But in the dark—" objected Thornton.

The second voice snarled, "Black Ops, you fool! Get out! Get out and don't ever return! Time waster!"

After he had finally managed to fumble his way out of the unseen door back into the world of light and visible shapes, a weak third voice floated up from the vicinity of the table.

"Another bloody spy!" it croaked.

THE BURNING EARS

Walls have ears, everyone knows that, but Thornton Excelsior still gasped in astonishment when he entered his new home and saw the fleshy organs growing in clusters in every room. Like oysters they were. Some of them, presumably the females, even had pearls, but those were just earrings and hadn't actually formed inside the ear.

Thornton scratched his head and pondered how he might best adapt to this situation. He had no intention of rejecting the house; it was perfect in every other way, with a superb view over the cliffs onto the beach, a roof garden, and a semaphore tower that enabled him to signal to passing ships on the horizon, should he be inclined.

He amused himself by strolling around his property, tugging the lobes of random ears or tapping them with a pencil. At last, on an impulse more serious than mischievous, he leaned close to a particularly hairy example and whispered into it, saying something about the ear itself, declaring that it was so hirsute it might tickle a hog.

The ear blushed, turned warm, began to throb.

Thornton was utterly delighted.

"So they really do burn when they are gossiped about! It's not merely a figure of speech. This is a discovery that once again affirms my status as a restless and original experimenter."

And he threw himself into a chair and chuckled.

On a desk, the telephone rang.

He snatched it up. "Yes? Ah, so it's you, Ursula. Indeed, my home is a dream; come and see it for yourself. You should wear the skimpy clothes this time and keep your hair loose."

He replaced the receiver on its hook and went into the kitchen to chop vegetables and cook a curry. The best way of persuading Ursula into his soft oval bed was with the old romantic appurtenances; she was that kind of girl. While cutting an onion he wounded his thumb, a minor injury but enough to make him shout, "Damn!"

The ears on the kitchen walls glowed and pulsed.

"Intriguing!" Thornton remarked.

So it wasn't only gossip that made them burn; simple curses achieved the same result. What else? He abandoned the chopping, selected an ear that was clean and whispered into it a secret he hadn't shared with anyone before, even his former wife. He said, "In meadows at night, when I'm on my own, I often pretend to be a cow."

Sure enough, the brightness of the ear increased.

Thornton clapped his hands in joy.

"What a perfectly superb way of saving money! I won't ever need to switch any of the electric lamps on."

And he had visions of himself sitting on his chair and reading a book and regularly calling out a vulgar oath or a perverse confession whenever the illumination dipped below a certain minimum level. Then he returned to his cooking and the hours passed.

Ursula arrived just after sunset. Thornton had been peering out of the window down at the beach, waiting for her to emerge from the ocean, but she never did that; he wasn't sure why he expected her to do so. She came up the road instead and rang the bell.

He flung open the front door and invited her in.

She was ravishing with her lithe form and freckles and he felt proud to be her host for the evening. He showed her into the dining room. The ears burned faintly, mysteriously, not too much, not too little, like radioactive mushrooms. He had confessed three or four minor indiscretions to adjust them to the most amorous luminosity.

She blinked. "A house lit by ears? How charming!"

Thornton attempted false modesty.

"Yes, but I didn't pay extra for them. All walls have ears; usually they are invisible and people aren't aware of them. For some reason, my home openly displays them. Unsure why I should be worthy of such an honour! When I say the right thing, they burn."

"You speak to them? What topics do you choose?"

"Secrets, obscenities, rumours..."

Ursula lifted an eyebrow. "Aren't you worried that the walls will share everything you tell them? That they will betray you to the government or to morality pirates on the high seas?"

And she flicked a damp glance out of the window.

Thornton laughed and poured wine. "How can they do that? There are ears in every room, thousands of them, but not one mouth. I can divulge the most intimate aspects of my life without undue risk. Speak no evil but hear plenty of it; that's their situation."

Ursula sipped her wine slowly and thoughtfully.

"If they are only able to absorb words but not release them, isn't there a danger they will explode?" she asked.

Thornton hadn't considered this possibility. He shrugged and finished the last of his curry. Ursula did likewise.

It was inevitable they would end up in bed together less than one hour later. The illumination in the bedroom had been set even lower than in the dining room; but in the throes of passion Ursula uttered so many sensuous and lewd phrases that the ears brightened rapidly. It spoiled the mood and a dismayed Thornton abandoned his task.

"No matter," she comforted him. "Try again later."

He nodded. "I'll go for a walk, get some fresh air, clear my head. Wait for me and don't assume I'm always—"

"I rarely assume anything," she replied sincerely.

He pulled on his trousers and slippers and trod off through interlocked rooms and onto the main balcony.

It was chilly outside. The waves lapped below and something creaked above. Twisting his neck he managed to see what it was. With a frown he realised the semaphore arms were in motion. What were they saying? He struggled to interpret the huge signals.

Then a drum of anxiety inside him was tapped with icicle sticks and he shivered all over. This was treachery!

The semaphore arms were relaying all his secrets, vulgarities, moans of love, to a dark ship on the very line of the horizon. He ran to fetch his binoculars and squinted through them.

It was a cargo vessel, a merchantman, and he could just make out the name, *SS Agony Aunt*, and the flag; it was registered in the federation of Zwieback. Hastening to his library to consult his encyclopaedia of ships, he learned the bitter truth and growled.

This vessel specialised in transporting mouths.

Empty mouths: that was normal.

But the semaphore arms were refuelling them right now; giving them all the salacious details they required to be full again, to set their tongues wagging like horizontal pendulums.

Clearly an illicit arrangement had been agreed between the house and the ship, namely the export of mouthfuls of salacious snippets to foreign gossip columns! This was a very lucrative international industry: Gossip Columns, together with Prattle Pillars, held up the roofs of every Scandal Stadium in existence, and every city had one of those arenas. Maybe this ship was sailing back to Zwieback?

The mouths would be unloaded there and milked in the stadium on a weekend afternoon. Some mouths would be paired off and forced to have arguments, to exchange obscenities.

Thornton cringed as he envisioned the tiers of spectators jabbing their thumbs up or down to the sounds of his romping with Ursula. No wonder the house had been sold so cheaply!

Well, he wasn't going to be exploited any longer.

He searched in every drawer and cupboard for wax or cotton wool, but couldn't find any; so in his desperation he snatched up a shiny new pair of scissors from the kitchen worktop and viciously began pruning ears from all the walls like a shortsighted barber.

THE GATES OF CORN AND TOFFEE

When drinking tea in company, posh people often elevate the little finger of the hand that holds the teacup, jabbing thin air with the tip of it. People who are posher might attempt to elevate other fingers too; the more posh, the more the number of digits raised. The poshest of all keep five fingers aloft, the teacup strapped to their wrist.

Thornton Excelsior wasn't posh, not especially so, and he preferred the taste of coffee to that of tea. He was prone to vivid dreams at night, sweet visions that left him with a bitter taste in his mouth on awakening. What a tragedy those wonderful nocturnal experiences never came true! That was his lamentation and it was an acute one.

He recalled an old legend about where dreams came from. Didn't they dwell in a celestial realm of constantly changing substance, a dreamscape that contained all potentialities, all hopes and fears? When the undreamed dreams were ready to enter the minds of human beings and other animals, they had to go through one of two gates.

Thornton winced as he racked his brain for details.

If the dream passed through the first gate, it would come true; but if it went through the second gate, it was false, a deceitful mirage. Yet he had forgotten what those gates were made of. He struggled to remember. The first gate was constructed of corn, wasn't it, and the second from toffee? It didn't sound entirely right but it would do.

None of his own dreams ever came to him through the gates of corn, only through the gates of toffee. He was thoroughly tired of this situation and resolved to do something about it. That's the sort of character he was, as uppity as a tectonic upthrust. He vowed to take legal action against his dreams in the highest court of the universe.

But he didn't know anything about that court, where it was, how to get there, or even whether it tried cases such as his; so he settled for a decent alternative, a court famed for its integrity…

The Court of Fictional but Very Serious Crimes is located near the site of the Ambient Pole, among the gentlest of our planet's poles, and anyone who can find their way to it and enter the dodecahedron that serves as the courthouse may seek justice there for free. Thornton eventually turned up and strode with a grimace into the building.

But a guard blocked his way and informed him that grimaces had to be left outside, unless it was a guide grimace.

Which it wasn't. So Thornton went outside and tied it up on the striped Ambient Pole and this time the guard let him pass into a long corridor. He walked with echoing footsteps — footsteps, footsteps, footsteps — until a door appeared in the wall. Obviously this was the door of a courtroom, so he opened it and stepped confidently inside.

Horrible forms flitted before his eyes: colours and shadows, some with depth and some without; solid musical notes bristling with icicles, thorns, stings and teeth; disembodied kangaroo legs jumped over him; a bird with cabbage leaf wings swooped at his head...

"Is this the court of false dreams?" he asked.

"No, it's the court of nightmares and it's currently in session, so please remove yourself instantly!" cried the judge. He kept his little finger in the air while striking his gavel on his desk.

"That's posh," Thornton said in surprise.

He returned to the featureless corridor and proceeded along it until he came to another door. Opening this and stepping inside, he found himself in another courtroom: dictators watched parades of soldiers marching off to war; bombs exploded; toxins billowed...

"This isn't the court of false dreams either," shouted the judge, "but the court of delusions of grandeur; it's in session, so shove off!" He kept three fingers in the air while striking his gavel.

"That's posher," Thornton said in astonishment.

"Out, out, out!" roared the judge.

Thornton obeyed, reluctantly but efficiently.

Once again he tramped the monotonous corridor until finally he came to a third door. And when he stepped through it, the judge didn't tell him to leave, so he realised he was in the right place at last. The judge looked at him and said, "Thornton Excelsior?"

"That's me. I'm the one who's looking for justice."

80

"You'll find it here. I am Judge Tapas." His gavel was strapped to his wrist and he kept all his fingers in the air.

"That's poshest," Thornton said in amazement.

"Yes it is," agreed Judge Tapas.

"I want to prosecute my dreams for being wrong."

"Often lie to you, do they?"

"All the time!" exclaimed Thornton.

The judge cried, "Call the first witness to the stand."

Immediately a vision appeared in the room, a tropical island lapped by gentle surf. Beautiful naked women drifted through the air and chocolate boulders rolled down the sides of edible mountains. Thornton drooled and stumbled forward, arms outstretched.

"Typical of your nightly dreams?" the judge asked.

Thornton nodded. "Yes, oh yes!"

"And that sort of stuff never happens for real?"

"Not once. Lies, all lies…"

Judge Tapas wasted no time delivering his verdict. "I see no need for more witnesses. It's clear you haven't been treated fairly. Not a single one of your dreams in the totality of your life has ever come true? That's not how the system's supposed to work."

"I'm very glad to hear that," gasped Thornton.

"I've consulted the original charter and a certain quota, not above 65% but not falling below 25%, of everyone's dreams must pass through the gates of corn before entering a head."

"It seems a generous amount," ventured Thornton.

"But 100% of yours have come through the gates of toffee. That's not acceptable. So I rule in your favour!"

"I only want my allotted share," sniffed Thornton.

"You will receive compensation!"

"You really mean to say that I've won my case?"

"Of course. Weren't you listening?"

"I'm overwhelmed by the verdict, your honour."

The gavel rose and fell repeatedly on the desk. And the desk vibrated and these vibrations somehow communicated themselves to Thornton and he began undulating; and his undulations turned into the fast throbbing of a powerful headache. He was in bed.

Slowly he sat up and the muscles of his face tightened.

"It was a dream, just a dream!"

Jumping out of bed directly into his slippers, he stamped with softened anger into the kitchen, where he took a jar of coffee and made a cup of it before deciding he preferred it as a jar; then he sat and brooded over what had happened, a corny cliché come true.

"Corny?" he mused to himself. "But it never came through the gates of corn, because it was a false dream. I didn't win my case. That dream came through the gates of toffee, unless—"

He slurped his beverage, relocating it into his belly. "I've had enough. This is the final straw!" he growled.

And he threw away the straw through which he had been drinking and pulled on his jacket; then he left his house, but without changing into his shoes, electing to remain a man instead. He headed straight for the Court of Fictional but Very Serious Crimes.

"Legal action is the only choice I'm left with! I'll prosecute this dream until it does come true. Wait and see!"

This time he left his grimace at home. He didn't have a leash for it. On his journey, somewhere in the vicinity of your own house, dear reader, he passed a gateway made of corn; on the cob it was, roasted and salted, but he didn't venture beneath its steaming golden lintel. Just as well really. It was the entrance to an impossible maize.

WHETHER THE WEATHERMAN

The most famous mad scientist of Munich was once asked to put his mind to a problem that had been bothering meteorologists for centuries, namely how to correct the inaccuracies of the average weatherman. "You want an improved model, nein?" he asked them.

They nodded in the affirmative; but they said that one model would be enough and that nine were unnecessary.

That was only the first misunderstanding. The reason they didn't speak German was because they lived in Wales. The most famous mad scientist of Munich had emigrated there long ago.

Nobody knew why, not even he: once he created a machine to tell him the answer but it didn't know either. "Not knowing either is all very well, and so is not knowing my Uncle Hans, but neither of those not-knowings help me in knowing why," he muttered.

Karl Mondaugen was his name, if you haven't guessed.

Anyway, he went back to his workroom and tinkered with components and fitted them together first one way, then another, then a third way and a fourth, then a fifth, sixth, eighth (why he missed the seventh way is still a mystery), until ultimately he succeeded.

He returned to his employers with his construction.

"Um," they said. "This is a robot."

"Ja, a mechanical weatherman, superior to the human kind, exactly the thing you asked me to invent for you!"

They shook their curly Welsh heads slowly.

"We wanted an improved model of the weather patterns; a method of more precisely modelling the weather, the changing barometric pressures, shifts in wind direction and other variables so that our forecasts would be less prone to error than they currently are."

"Only now you tell me!" bellowed Mondaugen.

"Wait!" retorted the meteorologists.

"For what?" cried the genius.

"Maybe we can still use your robot…"

"You are wondering whether the weatherman is any good?"

"That's it exactly. Well, is he?"

"Ja!" Mondaugen rapped his creation with his knuckles. "Without any doubt he is the finest weatherman in existence. Look at his skin: covered with solar panels! The sunlight that shines on him will generate electricity directly. Consider his rump region. He has no conventional buttocks but a turbine. His bum is a windmill designed to harness the currents of moving air that blow from behind! As for the top of his head: it catches the falling rainwater, which is always plentiful in these parts, and uses electrolysis to convert it into hydrogen and oxygen!"

"Um. Great. But can he predict the weather?"

"Predict the weather? Why?"

"Because that's what weathermen do."

There was a pause. "Is it?"

"Didn't you know that until now?"

"I assumed they were men *powered* by the weather… I can see I have made a mistake… My construction is useless to you… I have failed… I will return to the drawing board…"

"Please do. And kindly stay there this time."

After Karl Mondaugen had departed, one of the meteorologists, more curious than his blasé colleagues, experimented with the robot for a few idle moments, pressing it all over. His thumb flicked a concealed switch and the contraption sprang to life.

"I am Thornton Excelsior!" it croaked.

The meteorologist laughed.

"I am a man of great wealth and dubious taste."

They didn't believe that.

Then it ran out of the building before anyone could stop it. And that's how Mr Excelsior came into the world. He dines on the wind and the rain with as much relish as a gourmet slurps unicorn soup. But he never found much use for his solar panels in Wales.

NOTE TO ONESELF

"I'm afraid that your son," whispered the doctor in a sepulchral but mildly ironical tone, "has turned into a note."

"A note? I don't understand!" Mrs Excelsior gasped.

"A musical note, of course."

"I still don't follow you."

"It's perfectly simple. A crotchet."

Mrs Excelsior wasn't very musical herself. She gazed down at her boy and moved forward to cover his strange body with the bedsheets, but the doctor restrained her and murmured:

"Leave him exposed. It's more healthy that way."

"But a crotchet! What's that?"

"It's equivalent to a quarter of a semibreve in length."

"Is it catching? Is he contagious?"

"That depends on the tune."

"My poor Thornton!" sniffed Mrs Excelsior. She was flustered and hot and beads of sweat stood out on her brow like the spawn of some recently discovered and still unnamed amphibian; she retreated into the corner of the room and chewed on a knuckle.

"Medical mysteries and miracles *do* happen." Doctor Vaughan smiled but he kept his teeth concealed and his eyes remained cold. "So there's no point worrying yourself unduly."

"Do you have medicine for him, doctor?"

"Not really, no. How could I?"

Mrs Excelsior gestured at her son in despair.

Thornton remained immobile, a black flattened spheroid on the end of a long stalk, like the magnified spermatozoon of a grotesque mutant god, and his silence was pregnant with incredible tension, as if he was about to explode from the mouth of a cosmic trombone. There was something very repulsive and lonely about his form.

"Will he change back?" Mrs Excelsior stuttered.

Doctor Vaughan shook his large head with vigour and he felt suffused with a perverse professional pleasure despite the cramp in his neck as he exercised those atrophied muscles. "Far more likely that he'll fade away and vanish into nullity," he crooned.

"Into nullity? That sounds an awful destination!"

"Unless, of course," the doctor added quietly, "measures are taken to preserve him by fixing him to a stave."

"To a stave? Oh my goodness! Will that hurt?"

"No, no, no. Or just a little…"

Mrs Excelsior wrung her hands and self-pity filled her up from inside, as if a reservoir of the compressed stuff in her skull had been smashed and was pouring down into the hollow domestic vessel that she was. No husband to assist her in the hour of need; no relatives or friends to offer support; just herself and the grimy ornaments on all the shelves in every room in the damp crumbling house, the adjuncts of her hideous isolation. Even the neighbours had no sympathy.

This self-pity masqueraded as pity for the boy.

"My little mite, he never had a chance! Went off his food, he did, and then started to change colour, but the change was so rapid I didn't think to summon a doctor before now. Well, how could I have known? A musical note! It doesn't happen every day."

"They all say that," said Doctor Vaughan.

"What use will he be now?"

"That remains to be seen. Or heard, I should say."

"What will you do? What?"

Doctor Vaughan stroked his chin with a gloved hand. "Fixing him to a stave is essential, but first I must determine *what* note he is. Otherwise he could end up in the wrong position."

"But you know what note he is. You said a crotchet!"

"I mean what does he sound like?"

"He was a good boy, always softly spoken. That means he must be a soft note, doesn't it? A gentle note."

Doctor Vaughan removed his archaic hat, brushed the dust from the crown with his fingertips and said, "You don't really understand much at all, do you? There are many different notes in an octave and it is crucial that I determine which of them Thornton has become. The fact he has the appearance of a crotchet only tells me about his duration, and that only in relation to other notes in the same piece."

Mrs Excelsior was abashed. "I'm sorry, doctor."

He dismissed her apology with a curt wave. "I need to know his pitch. Is he A, B, C, D, E, F or G? Is he sharp or flat? He may even be a natural. Those are the important questions…"

"Will the answers make him more comfortable?"

"Yes, indeed; that's precisely the challenge that confronts me now. To find those answers! To make him 'better' is impossible, but to give him a chance to be happy with his new condition is a realistic aspiration, though it presents me with immense difficulties."

Mrs Excelsior squinted. "If he's a musical note, why can't we hear him with our ears, doctor? We're not deaf."

"Clearly he needs to be expressed properly first. If we take a published music score, maybe something by Debussy, 'Claire de Lune' for instance, we can read the entire document without hearing a single note. Musicians might hear the melody in their heads, but ordinary people will see just an array of black symbols on black lines."

At the same time he made this speech, he removed a stethoscope from the pocket of his frock coat and applied it to his ears; then he pressed the other end to Thornton's bulging head.

Frowning slightly, the doctor said, "He does have an inner vibration. I am no expert and yet I'm sure it is—"

Mrs Excelsior fidgeted as she awaited his verdict.

"D flat," he announced finally.

"Well, that's something to be grateful for, isn't it?"

The doctor held up a restraining hand. "I don't have perfect pitch, so I can't be certain. He'll have to be taken to the hospital where tests can be conducted that will confirm my verdict."

"Conducted? By a conductor, you mean, doctor?"

Doctor Vaughan sighed. He returned the stethoscope to his pocket and said gruffly, "There's no evidence to suggest he is a note in an orchestral work, Mrs Excelsior. He might derive from an example of chamber music or even an instrumental solo. How am I supposed to know to which opus he belongs or which composer wrote him? These may prove to be issues that can never be solved. Thank you."

Mrs Excelsior withered under his contempt, but some resistance deep inside her made her blurt out:

"Can't you name that note in one?"

"No, I cannot!" he spat. Then he rocked on his heels and added, "The main lack here is *context*. A note in isolation, however beautiful, has no inherent resolution. Only a melody can provide that. On his own, fixed to no stave, with no notes before or after him, Thornton is only a sound. His musical potential will be wasted until he finds his correct context. But do you appreciate how difficult

87

a task I'm confronted with? There have been thousands of composers in history!"

And he gazed at the wall, as if it was a window through which the past could be magically viewed; and Mrs Excelsior looked also, at the peeling wallpaper, and for long seconds they stood immobile, awaiting the parade of extinct geniuses that never passed.

Mrs Excelsior cleared her throat nervously. "Might he not be happy in *any* piece of music that uses a D flat?"

Doctor Vaughan scowled. "Think about that carefully. A specific D flat in a Bach fugue is *not* the same as a D flat in a work by Prokofiev or Rossini or Villa-Lobas, even though the pitch, duration, attack, decay and tone colour of the note might be identical. The context is what gives a D flat its unique character; and that context is a development through time. Music without time simply can't exist!"

There was silence in the bedroom for a minute.

"What now, doctor?" she asked.

"I will consult with a colleague of mine and then arrange for Thornton to be transferred to hospital. You are required to sign some papers. In the meantime I suggest you take these pills."

He passed her a little bottle that rattled sadly.

"To settle my nerves?" she asked.

"If you like," he concurred.

She nodded, submissive to the medical profession.

Doctor Vaughan removed himself from the room and the house, trying not to laugh aloud as he bowed under the low lintel of the front door and crunched down the short gravel path to his car. He didn't look back as he climbed into the driver's seat and started the engine. But he hummed as he rolled away, a medley of classical favourites, and his eyes shone with tears that themselves were like notes.

Mrs Excelsior remained in the bedroom, watching over her son with a vague feeling that she ought to be doing something more, making him a hot water bottle or cooling his smooth and featureless brow with a damp cloth. "My poor little boy, my crotchety son. D flat, the doctor said. And he knows best, he's a graduated man."

She resisted the urge to clutch him and cradle him in her arms. With a body as slender as a finger, he seemed too fragile. If only she had a stave at home! Then he wouldn't have to go to hospital, but could remain here, another fixture, overfamiliar and safe.

A brief squall lashed the window with rain. The drops ran down the grimy pane like notes at a loose end.

Doctor Vaughan drove through the gates of the hospital. He parked and went to see his colleague and rival, Doctor Frazer. A mutual hatred had grown up between the two men that was so comprehensive that it ensured they were tied to each other more closely than with the bindings of friendship. Very often they collaborated on unorthodox projects and experiments, hoping that some process would go drastically wrong and maim, annihilate or discredit the other.

"Another one," he said. "I'm sure there must be a pathogen responsible for these transformations, perhaps a virus in the shape of a note. Who can say? It's very noteworthy: my joke!"

"I say it's a genetic mutation!" cried Doctor Frazer.

Doctor Vaughan shrugged. "D flat."

Doctor Frazer frowned. "Shame. I need an F sharp to finish a nocturne that is proving to be very evocative."

"One of Chopin's, I presume?"

Doctor Frazer nodded; his taste in music was conventional enough, as was Doctor Vaughan's. Then he said, "Come and see the progress I have made in the past week. It's incredible."

He took a key and opened a hatch in the floor.

A spiral staircase wound down.

At the bottom was a narrow passage. Secure cells stood on either side and through the peepholes in the doors the inmates could be observed in secrecy. Dr Vaughan stooped and pressed his eye to the first hole. At the rear of the narrow chamber stood a tall wooden rack, and on the rack was an arrangement of five long skewers.

"A lively Mozart," he commented, tapping a foot.

Impaled on the skewers were living musical notes, crotchets, minims, semiquavers, writhing in agony, tails lashing impotently, screaming with an intensity of emotion that should have been utterly disturbing; but the result was melody, beauty from pain.

Doctor Frazer relished the role of official guide.

"And here we have a finished Brahms... A Mahler further along... A particular favourite of mine after that: Ravel... So you can see that I have been busy. The mutation is increasing."

"Because the contagion is spreading," said Doctor Vaughan.

"I can't accept your virus hypothesis."

89

"What does that matter to me?"

Doctor Frazer snorted; he quickened his pace along the passage to the end where stood a door larger and sturdier than its fellows. "I suggest we keep your D flat in here. In the cage."

"The cage!" Doctor Vaughan winced. "Anything new?"

"Why not judge for yourself?"

He peered through the peephole with distaste. The cage was the largest of all the cells in the hospital. Here the notes weren't fixed to any stave at all; they were free and able to interact randomly, to cannibalise, mutilate and mate with each other. It was pure chaos, a visual equivalent of chance music, discordant and nightmarish.

"Cacophony!" groaned Doctor Vaughan.

"But one day a coherent melody line will emerge," said Doctor Frazer teasingly. "Monkeys and bassoons…"

"Perhaps after millions of years. Can you wait?"

Doctor Frazer plucked at the elbow of his colleague. "Listen, I had an outstanding and unexpected result yesterday. Every note in the cage fell silent simultaneously and I timed the silence and it lasted for almost four minutes and thirty-three seconds…"

Doctor Vaughan had nothing to say in reply.

"That's music of a sort, isn't it? Coherent music? Negative but valid! I was delighted," urged Doctor Frazer.

"Too avant-garde for me, as you well know."

"And for me too, I suppose…"

"I've seen enough now."

They walked back down the corridor, tramped up the spiral stairway and locked the hatch carefully. Then they stood and regarded each other and licked their lips without hunger.

"What if we transform into musical notes also?"

"We're immune. The operation!"

"Are you sure it works?"

"Yes!" Like an angry lover, Doctor Vaughan unbuttoned his shirt and bared his chest; and Doctor Frazer did likewise. Jagged scars matched on each breastbone, the result of mutual surgery, for each doctor had taken it in turns to open his rival and reshape his heart with a scalpel. The organs were weaker as a consequence but strong enough; one carved into a bass clef and the other into a treble clef.

They collided slowly and rubbed chests together.

Like the cold hands of a mother.

SAID THE SPOOK

"I don't believe in ghosts," said the spook.

"You don't believe in yourself?" gasped the werewolf.

The spook nodded. "I lack self-esteem."

"Don't be silly," said the phantom, "a spook isn't the same thing as a ghost. Not the same thing at all…"

"I was a ghost once," sighed the vampire.

"What happened?" cried the ghoul.

"Well, it was like this…" began the vampire, and he proceeded to tell a garbled account of how he was once a poor miller in an earlier century who was murdered by bandits in the forest; then his spirit rose out of his body and proceeded to haunt the bandit chieftain, the one who had slit his throat, making the rogue's entire life a misery by actually possessing him and forcing him to act against his will.

The skeleton rapidly tapped an impatient foot.

"Shh!" hissed the ghoul, "you sound like a xylophone and I am trying to listen to the vampire's narrative."

"Yes, but he's drawing it out quite a bit, isn't he?"

"That's his privilege, of course."

"How come he gets your respect and I don't?"

"He's a Count; but what are you? Without a shred of flesh on you, I'd say you were merely a subtraction."

"That's a really bad play on words," sniffed the skeleton.

"So what? It's a good insult…"

"Stop bickering!" growled the werewolf.

The vampire was oblivious to all this fuss. He was explaining how his ghost possessed the bandit chieftain by entering into his brain through his nose; then he would force the miscreant to flop on the ground and writhe and grimace and do all sorts of humiliating things. The other bandits soon abandoned their leader in dismay and went elsewhere, leaving him in the mouth of a cave to be eaten by the mouth of a bear or whatever ravenous predator happened to come along first.

"Unfortunately," continued the vampire, his fangs gleaming in the pale moonlight, "I got trapped inside his brain. I lost my way among the tangle of synapses and couldn't get back out!"

"That sounds scary!" remarked the phantom.

The vampire nodded and his cape swished in the night breeze. "It was absolutely terrifying, I can assure you. I rushed hither and thither, trying to escape my prison, but I was stuck for good. So I decided to accept my fate and things got easier. I settled in and was gradually absorbed by the host body, until I *became* the bandit. Once this happened, I ventured forth and returned to my old ways, robbing travellers in the wood. But one dark night I chanced on the wrong victim."

"Who was it?" asked the spook.

"A werewolf! And he attacked and bit me!"

The werewolf looked sheepish. "Don't swivel your heads at me, I had nothing to do with it, honestly…"

"No, it wasn't you," said the vampire hastily.

"Maybe it was one of my cousins?"

"I have no idea who it was, but I only just managed to escape his teeth and claws before he devoured me; yet I was now infected, and so I turned into a werewolf myself every full moon. It was fun, in a way, but finally I was captured by hunters and killed."

"Did they shoot you with a silver bullet?"

The vampire shook his head. "They dragged me back to a quaint little village and burned me alive at the stake. Fire is another way of destroying werewolves. People came and toasted muffins. But when a werewolf dies it turns into a vampire, a fact that humans keep forgetting, and I soon got revenge on them! And that's who you see before you now: a vampire who was once a werewolf who was once a bandit chief who was once a ghost who was once a poor wandering miller…"

There was a long pause. The spook cleared its throat.

"So *you* believe in ghosts then?"

The vampire clucked his tongue. "Of course!"

"I still don't," said the spook.

"You don't believe what happens to be true?"

"No I don't. Why should I?"

The spook and vampire glared at each other. Before they started to bicker seriously, the phantom laughed to lighten the mood and said, "I knew a man who was the opposite of that."

"The opposite of what?" prompted the ghoul.

The phantom adjusted his ectoplasm.

"Opposite in attitude, I mean. He had no evidence for the existence of ghosts but he was a firm believer in them. His friends were sceptics and mocked him and so he needed to obtain proof to silence them. But in fact he required that proof for himself even more. His name was Mr Thornton Excelsior and he did everything possible to meet a ghost. He slept in old churchyards, went for midnight walks in lonely forests, used Ouija boards in the hope of contacting the departed."

"All without success, eh?" asked the werewolf.

The phantom rolled his insubstantial eyes in his wispy sockets, nodded and sighed. "Nothing ever worked."

"That's a shame," remarked the skeleton.

"It drove poor Thornton mad," continued the phantom, "and he toyed with an extremely nasty but foolproof method of achieving his desire. He would guarantee his own haunting by creating a horde of vengeful ghosts. He reasoned that if he deliberately and coldly killed a group of innocent people, the souls of at least some of his victims would want revenge; they would visit him to punish him and this mass haunting would confirm his faith in the reality of life after death."

"That plan seems desperate," said the ghoul.

"It does indeed," agreed the phantom, "but Thornton proceeded with it anyway. He concealed a homemade bomb on a ship and he stood calmly on the quayside and watched as the vessel sailed off and exploded. Water drenched him; but he was even more thoroughly saturated with joy, for it seemed certain now that he would be haunted. How could he fail to be? A dreadful act like that deserves retaliation."

"Did he get what he desired?" asked the vampire.

The phantom smiled a thin smile.

"No. Ghosts haunt human beings. That's the way it has always been, a tradition that goes back millions of years. By resorting to such grotesque measures, Thornton Excelsior had demonstrated his *inhumanity*. He was no longer sufficiently human for ghosts to recognise him. So as they rose from the hold of the sinking ship (some even rode inside the bubbles from their own drowning lungs) they didn't sense his presence; he remained on the quayside, unhaunted, denied the very thing he most wanted, and every single one of the free souls brushed past him. But he didn't feel, see, hear, smell or taste a thing. And his faith…"

"He lost it?" ventured the skeleton.

"It never came back," answered the phantom.

There was another long pause.

The spook spoke first. "That tale had a twist ending."

"Yes it did," replied the phantom.

The spook said, "I've got a twist ending too."

"I don't understand—"

"Would you all like to see it?"

The vampire, werewolf, ghoul, skeleton exchanged glances. Then they said together, "Why not? Go ahead."

The spook took a deep breath, extended its thin multi-jointed arms and started spinning. It span faster and faster, became a blur, a spiral of force, a miniature tornado. Then it whirled away through the trees, laughing and crackling with blue thunderbolts.

"I didn't anticipate *that*," admitted the phantom.

THE NOTORIOUS UNCLEMUNCHER

I summoned Hogwash and Bum Note to my office by pulling a rope and ringing a bell. It isn't the sound of the bell that reaches them but the fact that the clapper is a living man, bound tightly and suspended upside down. One of his arms is free and whenever the bell starts swinging he quickly lifts a megaphone to his mouth and yells, "Hogwash! Bum Note! Come immediately to the clubhouse before I am dashed!"

That generally attracts the attention of the explorers.

The reason why the man is imprisoned inside the bell is because he's a thief; many years ago he stole the bell curve itself, inconveniencing all sociologists on the planet, and we never got it back. Acting as a clapper is his penance and also a ringing endorsement of our justice system. Chime and punishment: please take note!

My office door banged open and the two most incompetent members of the Eldritch Explorers' Club stood there. "Come in!" I said. "For my name is Jorge I. Barra and by the authority vested in me, even though I don't wear a vest, I intend to send you on a mission—"

Suddenly Hogwash and Bum Note split apart. They had been standing very close together, touching along their vertical axes, and now I realised they were really a single individual dressed in a papier-mâché suit. Shards fluttered and settled and the man who loomed before me was triumphant and furious and perfectly familiar. Thornton Excelsior!

He said, "What do you mean by 'vertical axes'? I don't carry ancient weapons around with me, not even a sword, and if I did want to arm myself I'd choose a blunderbuss loaded with elbows and hands. Your peculiar slanders are un-axe-cceptable."

"I didn't say axes," I said. "I said *axes*."

There was a pause. There often is.

"You have abused your position as my temporary replacement," he finally growled, "and so I have come back to oust you and I came in disguise to fool your loyal readers out there. Get out of my sight at once!" Then he blinked. "But that's *not* an excuse to poke me in the eyes. You are banned from the clubhouse!"

And Jorge I. Barra left the office with his tale between his legs. And I sat down at his desk, for the first-person narrator has changed to Thornton, and he is me, as you can see.

I summoned Hogwash and Bum Note by pulling a rope and ringing a bell. The thief who was the clapper cried, "Not again! Was the bell curve really so valuable? I somehow doubt it."

My office door banged open and the two most incompetent members of the Eldritch Explorers' Club stood there. "Come in!" I said. "How did you get here so amazingly quickly?"

"This is our response to the first summons, not the second," they explained breathlessly. I was embarrassed.

"Ah yes, of course... But I don't care to discuss trivia with you. I am going to send you on a mission!"

"Is it dangerous?" they asked.

"Wait a moment, I'll check." And I skipped to the end of the story and read what was written there; then I came back. "No," I lied. I unfurled a map on my desk. "It's your task to find the Infamous Anteater and procure a signed photograph of it."

Hogwash and Bum Note leaned forward. "Where?"

"Take the left turn at this junction," I said, tapping on a portion of the map with a knuckle. "That's where the lair of the beast can be located. Take this camera and also this pen."

"What about funds for the journey?"

"Certainly. How much are you willing to pay me? Empty your pockets at once! Thanks and I'll keep the change, don't mind if I do. Don't dare return to the clubhouse without the photograph; and the autograph *must* be genuine. The Cosmic Mind, who is our ultimate employer, insists on this point. I suppose he wants it for his collection."

And I sent them away with an imperious wave. It lapped against the walls of the office and stained the wallpaper green; then it returned and floated my desk out of the open window. That's the last time I bid anyone farewell with an oceanic gesture!

Hogwash and Bum Note set off valiantly enough.

They trudged through the pre-dawn dark. Then dawn was born and it was light. How light exactly? Three pounds sterling and four fluid ounces, according to the midwife. The midwife? If *she* existed, there must be endwives too. The explorers peered in both directions but couldn't see them. A good thing, I suppose. Endives? Those are vegetables used in salads, aren't they? Let us continue properly…

At the junction they turned and soon entered a narrow valley and at the end of the valley stood a monster.

"Will you sign your photograph?" asked Hogwash.

"No," said the monster.

"After we have taken it," elaborated Bum Note.

"No," said the monster.

"Why not?" chorused the explorers.

"Because only the Infamous Anteater would agree to a request like that and I'm the Notorious Unclemuncher."

"I think we took a wrong turning at the junction," opined Hogwash, to which Bum Note added, "Eeeek!"

"Do either of you gentleman have a niece or nephew?" enquired the Notorious Unclemuncher quite politely.

"Not on us," responded the hapless pair. And that was true: they didn't. "Shall we," they wondered, "go in search of those aforementioned items on your behalf? We could set off on the quest promptly and we *promise* to return if we are successful."

But the Notorious Unclemuncher held up a claw in a sign of negation and opened his jaws in a sign of mastication and said through his nose, "You both seem avuncular fellows and that's sufficient proof for me. I think I ought to eat you without delay—"

A faint voice drifted up the valley, a summons that couldn't be ignored. "Hogwash! Bum Note! Quick!"

"Saved by the bell," muttered the Notorious Unclemuncher.

The explorers made their escape…

"I wonder who rang it?" gasped Hogwash as he ran up this incline towards the end of the story. "Perhaps it was the reader out there, the one who is grimacing at this sentence right now?"

"No, I just think it was a dreadfully contrived tactic by the author to avoid a proper ending to our mission," puffingly answered Bum Note. "He has done this sort of thing before."

"Dreadful contrivance? Yes, that rings a bell."

READ ALL ABOUT IT

He stopped at a kiosk to buy a newspaper and then he went to the park to read it. Other men sat on other benches with other newspapers. There was nothing unusual about that. Thornton Excelsior opened to a random page and scanned the first headline. GHOSTS AND WEREWOLVES DON'T EXIST! He read the story with a frown. It had been proven scientifically. There were no such things. There were only zombies and vampires *pretending* to be ghosts and werewolves. The scoundrels!

What was the world coming to? The next point on its orbit around the sun, of course, but apart from that... He turned the page. But Thornton never read newspapers the way most people did. He dived into the middle and then worked backwards to the front. The rear section he could safely ignore: it tended to be crammed with financial analyses and the results of rugby games. GIRAFFE SLEEP RIDDLE SOLVED! Having read the last story with a frown, he read this one with a smile.

Of all the land mammals on the planet, the giraffe requires the least amount of shuteye. As little as one hour a night can be sufficient. But how is this possible? It turns out that the neck of the animal is so long that it crosses several different time zones when it is extended horizontally. So the *same* sleeping hour can be enjoyed *multiple* times. That's logic. Yes, of a sort. Thornton winced and turned the page again. The newspapers do tend to exaggerate: that's an understatement.

A third headline caught his eye. MAN READS NEWSPAPER IN PARK! It seemed that an individual by the name of Hokey Raindrop was sitting on a bench and indulging his casual reading habit *at this very moment*. Thornton was shocked. A description of Mr Raindrop was given in the final paragraph of the story. Thornton gazed critically at the man sitting on the bench nearest to his own, who was holding a newspaper in front of his face, obscuring it. His hat and shoes matched the printed description.

Standing up abruptly, Thornton strode over to this fellow and took a proper look. "Are you Hokey Raindrop?" he demanded. The man nodded in the affirmative. "How dare you?" continued Thornton, hopping from one outraged foot to the other. The man protested meekly: he had done nothing wrong, he was merely passing the time of day. "That may be so," howled Thornton, jabbing at the man with an extended forefinger, "but I read about it in the newspaper. Filth!"

"What was written there?" asked Mr Raindrop anxiously.

"That you were brazenly reading a newspaper in the park! And when I came over to investigate I discovered that you were!"

Mr Raindrop shook his head. "No, no, that isn't accurate. Newspapers always exaggerate, distort or lie. I wasn't reading it, I was merely looking at the pictures. You shouldn't believe everything you read. And why be a hypocrite? You are more evil than I am."

"Do you have any evidence for that accusation?" shouted Thornton.

"The details are in here," answered Hokey Raindrop; and he waved his newspaper, which he had rolled into a tight cylinder, like the wand of a magician who conducts orchestras in his spare time. Thornton lunged for it and a brief tug-o'-war followed. Mr Raindrop wasn't very strong. He resisted valiantly but to no avail.

Thornton unfurled the newspaper. On the front page was a photograph of himself and the awful headline: EXCELSIOR STEALS NEWSPAPER! He fell to his knees and wept tears of shame.

"Don't worry about it," soothed Mr Raindrop. "If you read about it in the newspaper it's probably untrue."

"But I *did* snatch a rolled-up newspaper from you!"

Mr Raindrop frowned. "I don't think you did. I suspect it wasn't a rolled-up newspaper but the lever of a device. And I'm almost certainly the device in question. You can't trust the news."

Thornton squinted. His vision misted and then cleared. He was no longer in the park but in a subterranean bunker. The object in his hand really was the lever of a device, a lever that he had pulled; and the device was a bomb of unprecedented power, a doomsday machine.

It went off. The world exploded. Fragments of continents and globules of magma as large as oceans were flung through space. A newspaper floated in the vacuum, charred at the edges but still serviceable. The headline that glittered in the starlight declared: THORNTON DESTORYS HUMANITY!

The journalists had got it right at last.

PUTTING THINGS OFF

Suddenly, with one mighty bound, it was a dark and stormy night! Hold on a moment... How did that sentence end up in this story? I always pick clichés out of a text before I publish it, with a special fork designed for the task. This one in fact: Ψ. Any isolated cliché that resists forking can be destroyed by reversing its polarity; but that's easier said than done. More often than not, attempting to reverse the polarity of a cliché is like trying to get magma out of a heart...

Thornton Excelsior finally stabbed himself in the back once too often. Not with a fork but metaphorically. He has absolutely no loyalty to his future self, feels no empathy at all for the Thornton of tomorrow, his chronological successor, in the same way that his previous self, the Thornton of yesterday had no loyalty to the Thornton of today. He regards his future self as a being completely separate from himself, as little more than an unlovable neighbour.

This doesn't mean that he ever bears him malice: he simply has no particular interest in that fellow's welfare. "I don't care about the man I'll be tomorrow," he would say, "and why should I? Does *he* care about *me*? Of course not!" And so he lived in a manner that might be regarded as reckless or irresponsible but which in truth was perfectly consistent with reason and logic. For we *aren't* the same person tomorrow as we are today: this is real philosophy.

Everything about us that makes us what we are is mutable and transient. Our atoms, memories, location in spacetime: all are subject to constant change. Thornton Excelsior was no exception. But he acted in accordance with this insight, rather than simply acknowledging it as an intellectual fact that had nothing to do with his daily routine. Whenever he considered his situation in the world he realised it was the fault of a stranger, an unfriendly individual.

And that individual was his previous self, the Thornton of yesterday, who had unloaded onto *him*, the innocent Thornton of today, all the worries and responsibilities that he should have dealt with himself. Why should the Thornton of the present accept this burden? It was nothing to do with him. And so he too would pass it on: to the fellow in the following day who shared his name and identity but wasn't really him, the Thornton of tomorrow, an unsuspecting fool.

In this manner, Thornton kept putting things off.

Unpaid bills, awkward confrontations, relationship problems: they were passed onto him from someone else, his earlier self, even though he never asked for them and didn't want them. It was only fair that he, in turn, pass them on again, to his later self, also a separate individual. Otherwise he would be taking responsibility for issues that weren't his. And the moment he did that, he would become a pushover, a fall guy or patsy for all the prior Thorntons.

And yet he knew that one day it would be impossible to pass the buck further. The very last Thornton in the sequence, the Thornton who was living through the final day of his life, wouldn't have anyone else to unload the accumulated burden onto. He would be forced to sort it all out himself. Poor fellow! But why should the Thornton of today care about that? The Thornton of that final day didn't care about *him*. Unreciprocated sympathy is degrading.

But something had gone wrong. It turned out that the Thornton of today was the last one after all: this was the final day of his life. He was dying rapidly. Extreme old age was the cause, and the stress of worrying about dealing with all the problems that had been put off until now made a tangible pain in his chest, a clenched fist that throbbed and burned inside him, a displaced hand of doom. Those other Thorntons were traitors, ganging up on him!

He considered his predicament frantically but carefully.

There was only one way for him to avoid the accumulated responsibility and that was to stay alive until the next day. It was almost eleven o'clock, one hour to midnight. If he could only survive those sixty odd minutes, his present self would be safe and free: the Thornton of tomorrow would have to deal with the crisis, not him. With grasping fingers he picked up the telephone and dialled the local hospital. "I need a doctor! Send him immediately to my sickbed!"

"No doctors are available at such short notice, unless…"

"I am a man of great wealth and dubious taste. I can pay millions, do you hear? Millions! But he must be an ethical doctor. *Ethical*. This is very important. Your best ethical doctor!"

"Very well. We will send him by powerful motorbike."

And so they did, bless them.

The doctor arrived five minutes later; he pulled off his goggles and hastened to Thornton's side, checking the dying man's pulse, respiration, blood pressure and bank account. "Are you an ethical doctor?" mumbled Thornton during this process. "I once had dealings with two members of the medical profession, a pair of rogues, Vaughan and Frazer they were called, and they were most *unethical*. I don't need the kind of attention doctors like that can offer me. What are you?"

The newcomer stood erect and saluted smartly. "I am Dr Heelsnap Pinktoes, the most ethical doctor this side of bashful modesty. No doctor in history has been quite so ethical."

Thornton was satisfied. He explained his predicament and bewailed the landslide of tasks and responsibilities that had crashed down onto him from the past. Then he indicated the clock on the bedside table, uttered the words, "Until midnight!" and fell back exhausted on the pillows. Dr Pinktoes clucked his tongue, opened his medical bag and pulled out a contraption that resembled the collision of a thousand giant metal spiders. "Will that thing really prolong my life?" rasped Thornton.

"Prolong your life?" Dr Pinktoes was bewildered. "I don't know anything about such matters. I don't deal with health but with ethics. I'm an ethical doctor, which is what you asked for."

"Yes, but…" Thornton was too weak to protest properly.

Dr Pinktoes lowered the contraption onto his patient's bare chest. It adhered there, held firm by some strong electromagnetic or gravitational field. The multiple mechanical arms uncurled: they were extendable tentacles. A control was adjusted and the device hummed.

"The circuitry has been attuned to the frequency of your soul. These arms are operated by thought alone. Use them wisely."

"But my health…" wheezed Thornton.

Dr Pinktoes answered primly, "I am not here to fix your health but to cure your ethics. I am an ethical doctor. There is no time to lose: you know what needs to be done. I suggest you do it."

Thornton grimaced. Then he made a decision. The arms waved like the legs of an inverted beetle. Suddenly they speared through the open window, diverged out into the world, reached over houses, snaked out of the city and over the moors and oceans to other cities, entered rooms and offices. They paid unpaid bills, soothed mistreated girlfriends, cleaned dirty dishes in sinks, picked up dropped litter, wrote letters to neglected friends. An entire lifetime of deferred tasks. And then—

102

The clock struck midnight. Thornton Excelsior was dead.

Thirty thousand previous Thorntons, one for each day of his life, stared hard at this moment from the past. Then they pointed at the corpse and laughed, billowing the mists of time.

"I can't believe he fell for it. What a loser!"

THE CANAPÉS OF WRATH

The rusty doorbell tinkled like an orchestral icicle and Hogwash cried, "See who that is, will you? I'm busy cooking!" And Bum Note tramped along the corridor like a chamber hobo — please note the three vagrant puns in that sentence — and flung open the portal.

"I am the Cosmic Mind," answered the unexpected guest.

"But— you look like a— donkey!"

"Yes, yes, this is my habitual form when on Earth. I am paying a random visit to all my agents in every dimension."

"In that case, come inside..." said Bum Note nervously.

The Cosmic Mind trotted over the threshold and down the passage into the living room. "Am I interrupting anything?" he asked as he stood near the sofa and gazed around. The zoetrope was off; the puppets had wilted; the other ornaments were slowly turning themselves inside out. But none of the neglect was wanton. The two inhabitants of this house were explorers and therefore often absent. It was to be expected.

"No, no, we're planning a little party, a soirée, later: to celebrate our return from Mizunderstan, a land full of incomprehensible... incomprehensible... Well, I don't rightly know how to describe them..."

"Things?" ventured the Cosmic Mind.

"Sort of. But not quite," replied Bum Note, and then he cupped his hands around his mouth and yelled, "Hogwash! Come here quick! We have a guest, a very important one. Drop what you're doing—"

"A guest?" growled the voice from the kitchen. "But it's too early! The party doesn't start for another two hours; I haven't finished preparing the canapés yet. It's not Thornton Excelsior, is it? Tell him to go away and come back at the correct time, will you?"

"It's not Thornton. No, in fact it's our employer..."

There was a loud crash, soggy and brittle at the same time. "I've dropped what I'm doing and I'm on my way!" Hogwash appeared, covered in flour and culinary stains, and gaped at the donkey.

"Please sit down, both of you," said the Cosmic Mind.

They did so, on a single armchair, hugging each other for comfort and to minimise their combined size between the two furnished arms that acted as barriers. Then they blinked furiously.

"Don't sack us!" pleaded Hogwash.

"We always did our best!" added Bum Note.

"Calm down, boys," soothed the Cosmic Mind, raising a hoof for silence and twitching his immense ears. "What manner of talk is this? You are explorers, that's hardly a secret, and I know you must be more thick-skinned than you are pretending to be…"

They stared at him mutely and glistened their chins with drool.

"You are explorers," repeated the Cosmic Mind, "and I am your patron. So why don't we do a little exploring together, eh? Why don't we, for instance, *explore* a few of our options?"

"Options?" echoed Hogwash and Bum Note.

"Yes indeed. I have no intention of making anyone redundant without ensuring they are fully prepared for alternative employment. Nothing is certain in this life of ours, my friends; and job security is an illusion easier to pop than a bath time bubble. The crucial thing—"

"So we've lost our jobs?" blurted Hogwash.

"In the wake of our greatest triumph!" wailed Bum Note.

The Cosmic Mind sighed and stood on his back legs, resting his front hooves on his hips. He was imposing and silly, an unusual combination. "As I was saying," he said, "the crucial thing is to be adaptable. I've had a think about it and I'm fairly sure I know what's best for the pair of you. There's no reason to get upset about anything."

"But we were planning a party. I made canapés and sent out invitations. I don't feel like celebrating now," sniffed Hogwash.

"Thornton Excelsior is coming; and Tarka the Rotter, Professor Vokisrep and The Cheeky Monkey too; plus Jorge I. Barra and the Infamous Anteater; not to mention Sir Jasper, Dr Miasma, Brinydeep, Lux, Glo, Tonguewaggle Chipchop, Pollux Jenkins and a dozen others. It's too late to cancel!" groaned Bum Note, his tears squirting cartoonishly.

The Cosmic Mind said nothing for many minutes. His jaw was clenched tight and he appeared lost in abstract rumination. Then he grinned and said, "Boys! Who said anything about giving you the shove? You've got the wrong end of the celery stick. I want to *promote* you."

"Promote us?" gasped the incredulous pair.

"Sure! For your incredible services over many exploits, I hereby elevate you both in status. You are explorers no longer!"

"But that means—" they protested.

"Exactly!" brayed the Cosmic Mind. "You are now ex-explorers, in other words fully accredited *plorers*."

"Plorers?" They were dismayed.

"Aren't you satisfied with that?" asked the Cosmic Mind.

"Well, what exactly does a 'plorer' do?"

"What an explorer no longer does. Isn't that obvious?"

"It should be. But—"

The Cosmic Mind narrowed his eyes to a squint. "You're starting to sound like an *implorer* now, Hogwash!"

"Personally I think it's outrageous that we—"

"And you, Bum Note, are starting to sound like a *deplorer*..."

There was a menacing pause.

"Very well," said Hogwash and Bum Note meekly. "We accept."

The Cosmic Mind nodded and came to rest on all fours again. "Good. I knew you'd see sense eventually. I hope you do a lot of successful and lucrative ploring in your new careers. I won't stay for the party. I have many more agents to visit tonight."

And he trotted back down the corridor and showed himself out.

Hogwash and Bum Note were crestfallen.

"How will we behave with propriety when the guests arrive? I don't think I can put on a brave face," said Bum Note.

"Me neither," agreed Hogwash, "but I have an idea that will liven up the party and take our minds off our melancholy. Why don't I dip the canapés in raw emotion sauce before serving them?"

"Raw emotion sauce! But that was banned years ago..."

"So what? We are plorers, remember? Plorers can get hold of unobtainable stuff: in fact that's the definition of a plorer that I invented just now! Raw emotion sauce! Pure liquid fury!"

"Yes!" cried Bum Note. "Yes! Let's do it!"

And they did. And it worked too.

But that's not another story...

THE PLUG

"I once met a succubus on a trolley bus," said Thornton Excelsior to Captain Dangleglum one morning, and the old sailor shrugged his shoulders, adjusted the neck of his blue sweater, filled his clay pipe with tobacco as dark and sticky as molasses and replied:

"With me, it was the other way around…"

Thornton blinked. "Meaning?"

"I once met a trolley bus on a succubus. Many years ago, it was, when Switzerland had a coastline and I was able to dock my ship in Geneva. I wandered along the elegant streets for an hour. Then a succubus pulled up alongside me and so I jumped aboard!"

"Oh yes," he continued, lighting his pipe with a short match, a Swan Vesta, and puffing furiously. "I know it might seem strange jumping on an unfamiliar female demon without asking any questions first, but it *was* an official succubus stop. She was enormous and transparent and strode along faster than a man could run."

And he flicked the dead match idly at Thornton, who stepped out of the way and remarked dryly, "When the unhappy workers at the Swan Vesta factory went on strike there was a terrible blaze…"

But Captain Dangleglum wasn't really listening and he blew a smoke ring and continued his reminiscence: "I entered through a hatch in her belly. There was only one other passenger in the carriage and that was the trolley bus I mentioned. I wondered if the succubus had swallowed it for her lunch, but no! it was a proper fare-paying commuter."

"A sentient trolley bus? How peculiar!" cried Thornton.

"Indeed. We began chatting."

"I'm surprised you had anything in common!"

"Well, it was just small talk, the weather, the gladiator results, the stock and broth exchanges, taps."

"Taps? I rarely bring those up in casual conversation."

"Too bad. Anyway, the trolley bus revealed a secret to me. Although it was travelling to work at the Immigration Office, where it was a clerk, it had another job: an illegal occupation unknown to the authorities. On the sly, it transported commuters of its own! How about that?" Captain Dangleglum's pipe went out as he spoke.

"Your tobacco is too moist," commented Thornton.

"Yes, I prefer it that way. But listen: my story isn't finished yet! I asked the trolley bus if it was carrying passengers at that very moment and it replied in the affirmative. Two of them! They thought they were on a regular trolley bus, not an unlicensed decommissioned vehicle that was inside a giant succubus. So I pressed my face to the nearest window."

"And what did you see?" prompted Thornton obligingly.

"Just as the trolley bus said, a pair of blithely unaware commuters sitting in a carriage talking to each other! They were so absorbed in conversation that they didn't notice me peering at them. One was male, the other female. She was a demon, a succubus in fact. And he—"

"Was me," whispered Thornton with a shudder.

"Small odd world, isn't it?"

Thornton decided to change the subject. He slurped his cappuccino, blew the muddy froth off his lips and said, "Are you still smuggling angels or have you switched to some other product?"

"No, I don't bother with angels now. Religious contraband of any kind is more trouble than it's worth. The prophet margin — I mean profit, of course — is too small to make the risks acceptable to me." Captain Dangleglum emptied his extinguished pipe into his mug of overproof rum, swirled it around and gulped it down with a grimace. "Yum!"

Thornton flared his nostrils in mild disapproval. "What cargoes do you carry instead? Emotions? Monsoons?"

Captain Dangleglum waved his hand. "I'm finished with all that tricky stuff. Too fragile and unreliable and I nearly caught pneumonia with those teardrops and raindrops sloshing around. The only merchandise I smuggle these days is deserted beaches."

Thornton's eyes lit up. "Beaches? What kind?"

"Tropical, subtropical, temperate."

Thornton picked up his coffee mug and gestured with it at the street and the pedestrians and bicycles moving along it. "I miss the beach. Honolulu isn't what it once was. Do you remember when Hawaii was a chain of islands in the middle of the ocean? Those days seem to belong to a different world." He frowned. "Maybe they did."

"Which different world?" asked Captain Dangleglum.

"I don't know. Some alternative Earth, I suppose. I'm not in the mood for cosmological speculation right now. But tell me: do you sell any of those beaches to individual customers?"

108

"Not normally, but I might be willing to make an exception in your case. I have a sample with me, if you'd like to see it." And at Thornton's eager nod, the old sailor reached into an inner pocket of his coat and drew out a cylinder that gently rasped.

"It's rolled up in a scroll!" cried Thornton.

"Of course it is. You don't imagine I wander the streets with a fully extended tropical deserted beach, do you?"

"May I untie it here?"

"Absolutely not! You'll get me into dreadful trouble. Take it to a private spot away from the traffic and try it out alone. If you like it, you can pay me the next time we meet. If you don't, just return it in good condition and I won't charge you."

"That's what the rhino said to the bishop…"

"I beg your facile pardon?"

"Just a little joke." Thornton squirmed on his seat.

Captain Dangleglum had nothing more to say, so Thornton summoned the waiter and paid his bill, then he shook hands with the sailor and left the café, walking home as fast as his feet were able, the beach tucked neatly under his arm. When he reached his apartment block he tramped up the stairs to the roof and paused to thickly pant.

Yes, this was the perfect location to unroll the beach. It was a flat roof and though it was communal to every resident in the block very few people ever came up here. Thornton untied the green ribbon and snapped out the beach like a very broad whip: for an instant he was an exotic rug merchant demonstrating his wares in an eastern bazaar. But the pile of *this* carpet was yellow and white sand.

The smuggler hadn't deceived him. As the beach settled down, Thornton whistled through his teeth, a note as golden as a toffee, and kicked off his shoes. It was a strip of paradise, a beach that vanished beyond the limits of his vision. "Exquisite!"

He took his first step, felt the grains pour between his toes, then began striding like a castaway. Crabs scuttled out of his way, seabirds took flight, a row of angels played tunes.

Angels! What were they doing here? He frowned.

Six of them in a line, wearing sunglasses, haloes tipped at jaunty but still sufficiently divine angles. Five of them plucked harps; the sixth puffed a didgeridoo. There's always one maverick in any heavenly host. Thornton stopped before them and sniffed.

One of the angels shouted above the music, "Dangleglum transports the untaxed beaches in the same space where he used to store angels. Some goods always get lost down there, some bads too, in the hold of his ship. We fell out of our crate and lay in the darkness for weeks. When he loaded the beaches on top of us, we got stuck to this one…"

"That's fine," said Thornton, "but please keep the noise down."

He walked on, sweat sprouting.

The tide was low and the sea was far out, very far, too far. It didn't seem natural. Come back sea! He kept going, but instead of plodding in a direction parallel to the coast he headed directly for the surf. He fancied a swim, a cooling of his skin. Dead fish appeared and he stepped over and between them.

"It stinks! Why does the sea keep receding?"

Then he found it. The plug…

It had been pulled out deliberately. By whom?

The size of an ancient warrior's shield, with a chain as thick as his leg, it lay in the sand like a bad sculpture of a jellyfish. The plug that stopped the sea draining away into the centre of the Earth! So this was the real reason for low tides. All that stuff about the pull of the moon was a lie. Thornton swallowed.

What should he do? It was too heavy for him to shift by himself. No good asking the angels to help: they were too feeble for such work. He had no choice but to leave the plug where it was.

He increased his pace, lurching towards the disappearing line of foam-flecked blue. It was going out faster than he could move. Soon there would be only a desert, a featureless expanse of flat sand dotted with the decaying bodies of stranded starfish in unlucky constellations.

He began running, trying to match the speed of the retreating sea. Soon he was sprinting, arms pumping furiously but pumping only air, not water. And yet his desperation was ebbing too: it seemed he would reach the surf in the next minute and be able to plunge into the waves. How soothing the liquid would be on his aching metabolism…

Something in the distance broke the surface of the water. It was a giant tap. As the level of the sea around it fell, Thornton saw that it was larger than a man, bigger even than a horse or private helicopter. In fact it was the most massive tap in the world, identical in all other respects to an ordinary bathroom faucet. The tap of taps!

It stood on the apex of a very high pipe, a pipe with a diameter the same as his body, so that to climb it would be akin to hugging himself; but when the sea had vanished completely and the entire pipe was exposed, he knew that climbing it was his only ethical option.

Thirty metres or more it reared out of the sand into the cobalt sky and Thornton was determined to haul himself to the top, to turn the handle and make the tap mouth gush: to refill the sea. High tide, low tide, plug and tap. The secret was revealed at last.

Up he went, painfully slowly, gritting his teeth, spitting out grains of sand that tasted like his own tongue. Several times he slipped back a few metres, but he didn't fall. At last he reached the summit, grasped the vast handle and exerted his entire strength on it. With agonising slowness it creaked and turned: there was a trickle.

The trickle turned into a flood but Thornton didn't stop turning until the tap was opened to its maximum extent. The pipe that supported the brass monstrosity rumbled and shook with the force of the rising column of pressurised water inside it. A deluge.

He was exhausted. He straddled the roaring tap and rested.

"That Dangleglum sold me a dud!" he fumed. Then he recalled that he hadn't paid for the beach yet. Nor would he.

He closed his eyes and attempted to doze but the sound and fury of the waterfall jangled his nerves too much. The sea level was rising again, very quickly, and the base of the pipe was already lost beneath the agitated surface. With a start, Thornton realised that he was marooned on his perch, cut off on an island shortly to be overwhelmed.

Grasping the handle, he tried to turn the tap off; but it wouldn't budge. It was stuck fast. He groaned at the irony of the situation, then he remembered that groaning at irony only encourages it, so he rolled his eyes instead. And now the water level was halfway up the pipe.

The sun went down over the horizon of the rejuvenated ocean but its fruit stain reflections no longer delighted him. He was waiting patiently for the end. The sky darkened, the stars came out, the sea lapped higher and higher, it flicked at the toes of his dangling feet, washed over his ankles. He had only a minute or two before he was fully submerged.

The moon rose over the sea, rumbled towards him. It was orbiting at top speed, out of control perhaps, or simply in a hurry. Directly over him it passed, but too high for him to touch. Then a hatch opened in one of the craters and a passenger leaned out.

She was an enormous and transparent succubus...

"Hush! I'm moonlighting!" she hissed down at him. Then she cast a rope ladder in his direction and he snatched the lowest rung as it cracked straight for an instant. The moon continued racing: he was yanked off the drowning tap and into the soft night air.

"A single fare back to reality!" he cried.

And somewhere far below, the distinctive drone of a didgeridoo turned into a spluttering of bubbles, while in a different cosmos entirely an old sailor with useless tobacco made small talk about taps to his next casual acquaintance under the light of a gridlocked moon.

THE QUEUE

The Old Woman who lives in a Shoe converses in a thick Irish brogue. Little known fact. Thornton Excelsior didn't know it but he was happy to remain ignorant of the characteristics of people who dwelled in modest items of footwear.

He was a snob, a man immensely proud to possess a boot as his abode. The thigh's the limit when you live in a boot. Every single day he ran the risk of puns on the words 'tongue', 'heel' and 'sole' with the same smug smile on his face.

One morning there was a knock on the flap that he had cut into the side of his house and he answered it as if it was a proper front door. "Yes? How may I help you?"

"I'm sorry to point out, sir, that you jumped the queue."

Thornton blinked. "Pardon?"

"The queue, sir! You jumped it. Way back when."

Thornton licked his lips and struggled with an uneasy feeling that the face of his unwanted visitor was familiar. The problem was that it *shouldn't* be familiar: it was too wrong for that. It had been put on inside out or back to front and really was hideous.

"Have I met you before? Your name wouldn't happen to be Legitimus Blarney, by any chance?"

"Nope," replied the ugly stranger.

"But I'm positive I know you from somewhere…"

"Doubtless you do, sir. It was back in the queue, that's where. I am Grincrack Buncle and you jumped the queue and got the last normal face. I've been tracking you down ever since."

Thornton rubbed his chin. "The queue, you say? What queue are you referring to exactly? There have been so many."

"The queue for qualities and characteristics, sir. The queue when we all stood in the embarkation hall. Before we were born. Surely you haven't forgotten that? Lots and lots of queues, thousands of them, millions! Parallel lines. In Heaven, sir."

Thornton clucked his tongue sceptically. "That's all superstition, my dear chap. Heaven indeed! I don't believe in such a place. I'm too modern for all that nonsense: I live in a giant boot! Look at it. Why don't you take your peculiar ideas to the Old Woman in the adjacent valley? She's gullible in the extreme."

"I already visited her on the way here. She gave me directions to your boot. A helpful and friendly hag."

"But she lives in a shoe! She must be a dullard!"

Grincrack shook his head and said, "I saw no evidence of that, sir, but I can report that she's dreadfully skinny."

"Thin? Really! I had no idea."

"Oh no, sir. She's fat, grossly so, but she has got lots and lots of excess skin: ergo she's skinny!"

"Hmm, maybe she jumped the queue when they were handing out the skin?" ventured Thornton spitefully.

But Grincrack missed the irony. "Yes indeed sir! So you *do* recall the queues? And the queue for faces: you jumped it. You ended up with the face that was meant to be mine."

"I was jesting," sighed Thornton.

Grincrack looked at him reproachfully. Then he said, "How can you not believe in Heaven, sir?"

"Because religion is stupid and foolish and silly." Thornton grinned without mirth. "And daft and bonkers and ridiculous," he added. Then he took a deep breath. "Consider this. *An eye for an eye, a tooth for a tooth.* If true, dentists are in big trouble!"

"But that's just a saying, sir. Just a saying. Here's another. *When in Rome do as the Romans do.* Sounds reasonable, doesn't it? But what if it turns out that Romans never follow the advice of sayings? What if they always do the opposite of such advice? What if *that* is what Romans do? What then?"

Thornton mulled the paradox; he added the cinnamon, nutmeg and cloves of doubt to it and when it was properly mulled he poured it away like an unwanted tipple. "Your point is?"

"Sayings aren't religion, sir. Not by themselves. That's my point, sir, make no mistake about it. You jumped the queue, sir, and took the face intended for me and I was forced to improvise." Grincrack seemed on the verge of tears. Curious because it had always previously been a grass verge. "To improvise *this* mug."

Thornton winced at the use of slang. He always did. "Well, I don't intend giving you mine in exchange."

"But why not? Why not, sir? It's only fair!"

"It won't come off for one thing," answered Thornton, thrusting his hands into his trouser pockets to demonstrate how calm he was even when confronted with the most outrageous demands.

114

"And before you start lecturing me on modern surgical techniques, permit me to spare you the trouble. I'm allergic to them."

But the stranger wasn't dismayed in the slightest and in fact he began emptying his own pockets on the threshold. "It won't come off for one thing? Then maybe it will come off for *two or more*. Look closely, sir! I have many things. Take your pick."

Thornton sneered at the growing pile of junk. "A fossilised bolt of lightning? A comb with tusks instead of teeth? A bottle of sweat? These items are utterly useless to me."

"Not any old sweat, sir! It's the sweat of the world, sir! The perspiration of our planet! Sniff it…"

Thornton picked up the bottle, pulled out the cork and moved his nose into the rising vapours. "Ugh! It has gone off! Geo-B.O. That's not for me, I'm afraid. No thanks."

Grincrack continued to delve and extract. "A pancake, sir? A little mouldy but not too bad. It was Pancake Day last week and I made a dozen in honour of Pan, the god of pancakes, or as he is known in the ancient Sasquatch tongue: Fläppjàqq. This is the last one left, sir. Doesn't it tempt you even a bit?"

Thornton shook his head. He was growing tired of this farce. He wanted to return to the interior of his boot and enjoy a nice nap in a comfy chair. "My final judgment on the matter," he said, "is that you were at fault for allowing me, if that's actually what happened, to jump the queue and take the last face. The responsibility is yours, not mine, and I feel no guilt whatsoever. Let's face it, no pun intended, the queues were there to be jumped…"

Grincrack clenched his jaw and spoke in a voice that would embarrass a ventriloquist's dummy. "No pun intended? I hate it when people say that. Try harder next time. Puns should always be intended!" And he stamped his clumsy feet.

The items that had formerly belonged to his pockets were trampled to bits. Thornton watched them through hooded eyes. "Send your luck back to your supplier if you think it's tough."

"I make my own!" growled Grincrack.

"Let me tell you a story," said Thornton after a suitable pause. His gestures didn't match his words: that was the way he liked it best. "One of those queues was the queue for patience. I remember standing in line, waiting my turn."

Grincrack raised a weird eyebrow. "You *do* remember?"

115

"Yes, yes." Thornton nodded but his fingers wagged and waved. "And after standing in that line for ages, waiting for my allocation of patience and finally reaching the counter, who should jump in front of me? It was you. Yes, you! You took my quota of patience, the patience intended for me, and when it was my turn again, they had run out of it! The very last sachet of patience… Gone!"

"I-I-I," stuttered Grincrack. "B-b-b—"

"Don't try to apologise, it won't do any good. I don't have the patience to listen to your explanations and justifications. I never had it. You stole it from me, you funny-faced felon! And now you come here, to my boot, and demand that I face you my hand — I mean hand you my face? Despicable! The barefaced, or faceless, cheek of it. Hmm, maybe 'cheek' isn't the right word."

Grincrack Buncle was aghast, astonished and overawed. "I really don't know what this means," he croaked.

"It means we're evens," said Thornton. "Quits."

"I don't feel that we are."

Thornton shrugged. "Too bad." He yawned. "I can't stand here all morning. I have some dreaming that needs to be finished. There's something that has been bothering me for a long time, a question, and I can't find the answer in my waking life and so—"

"I'm not leaving with nothing," asserted Grincrack.

"My face remains in place."

"Then I demand another object as a substitute!"

Thornton pondered. "Very well." When he mulled an issue, it was vital to add the spices of scepticism, but not when he pondered it. "Wait here a moment." He went inside the boot and emerged a short time later with a rolled-up rug. He offered this gift.

"A carpet?" cried Grincrack. "Is that all?"

"It's a portable road, you fool."

And Thornton unrolled it with a flick of both his wrists. Off to the far horizon it trundled and over. It crossed the dusty plain and passed between mountains on the way. It was blue but not wet. A fine narrow road for a traveller, for a face seeker.

"You have all the patience that I don't," Thornton explained, "and so you are patient enough to continue your quest even though you know it is completely futile. Farwell! Toodle-pip!"

Grincrack hesitated, then he took his first step on the portable road. Thornton watched him dwindle. When he was no larger than the shoe of a shrew, he rolled the carpet after him, an accelerating cylinder with a diameter that increased on every revolution. It was a portable road, after all, and shouldn't be left as a permanent geographical feature.

Thornton returned to his comfy chair and settled down for a nap. He programmed his dreams by mumbling the question his conscious mind was unable to answer: "Why are wise men good but wise guys bad?" Then he lovingly said goodnight to his face.

FOSSILS

When Thornton Excelsior went on a camping trip to the coast, he took two friends with him. Paddy Deluxe hefted the tent and sleeping bags; Frothing Harris was the bearer of the pots, pans and food. As for Thornton: he carried himself with dignity because he preferred to travel light. And speaking of light reminds me to point out the lighthouse in the distance, a white tower that winks seductively at passing ships, proving that it is not a fossilised bone but a deliberate structure raised by men.

At the foot of a vast boulder near this lighthouse, the three explorers decided to make camp. They were protected from the wind here and it was a quiet spot where a cooking fire could be lit that wouldn't inconvenience anyone else. They unburdened themselves of their luggage and went to search for fossils in the jumbled rocks of the collapsed cliffs. This region was famous for the abundance of its petrified creatures and plants from an ancient time and it was not unheard of for collectors to find new species.

None of the trio were real collectors but they were interested enough in the subject to persevere for several hours. Each of them discovered something unknown, peculiar and baffling. Thornton chanced upon various rectangular objects, perhaps a variety of bivalve mollusc similar to the razor shell but much wider; Paddy found a row of neat holes, the footprints of a creature with tiny hooves; Harris located a few circular entities, possibly jellyfish, and also an oval creature with a stubby tail. That was enough.

Then they relaxed in front of their tent and prepared a meal, speculating on the lives of beings that had such curious forms. How must it feel to have a square or round body? Thornton leafed through several books of fossils in a bid to identify them, but without success. Then he threw the books down, admitted defeat and suggested a game of cards. They played until the sun went down, then they opened a bottle of rosé wine and passed it round until it was all gone. Bedtime followed and dreams of the far future.

Millions of years later, three bizarre lifeforms were exploring the same region. The continents had drifted apart and clashed together again and the geography was very different. The site was now far inland. Humanity had been extinct for a long time and the lighthouse had utterly vanished, reduced to dust that had blown away in gentle winds. One of the lifeforms called out in joy, "I have found some rectangular objects, perhaps a variety of bivalve mollusc. They are roughly the same size but of different thickness." His name was Thxqzton.

"Good for you!" commented the second lifeform. "And I have found a row of neat holes, the footprints of a creature with tiny hooves." His name was Pqxvvy and he mopped his brow with a tentacle.

"As for myself," said Haxvqss, the third lifeform, "I have discovered a few circular entities and an ovoid with a stubby tail. Shall we return to our tent now? I am starting to feel hungry…"

And that's what they did. They prepared a meal together, read books, played cards, drank wine. Or rather, they did the future equivalent of those things, and bedtime followed and dreams of the past's past.

For millions of years earlier, millions of years *before* Thornton and his two friends had camped at this spot, other explorers had visited the region. Three of them had arrived and pitched a tent, had read books, played cards and shared a bottle of wine around a campfire. Or rather: the prehistoric equivalent of those things. And just before bedtime one of them had said, "Imagine what might happen if we abandoned our equipment tomorrow and went home without it and it all turned into fossils?"

"That's a silly notion, Thorgryx," chided Paddarrrz.

"No, it's not. I think it would be a fine joke. Our books and playing cards would resemble a variety of bivalve mollusc; the holes made by our tent pegs might look like the footprints of a creature with tiny hooves; our pots and pans would leave circular impressions similar to jellyfish."

Paddarrrz shook his head and turned to the third explorer. "What do you think, Harralaghhas?" he enquired.

Harralaghhas scratched his nose with a claw and cast aside the empty wine bottle and answered, "I suppose I've just discarded an oval creature with a stubby tail? No, it's pure nonsense, I'm afraid."

Thorgryx sighed. "I guess you are right. It's about as likely as finding that a lighthouse had sprung up over there." He gestured.

And the three dinosaurs laughed at this for a long time.

119

THE HEAT DEATH OF MR UNIVERSE

One afternoon, Thornton Excelsior decided to take his old bicycle for a spin. And then, when it was sufficiently giddy, he mounted it and set off at high speed towards the far end of this sentence, but the brakes of the machine were faulty and he ended up skidding beyond the full stop into the margin, right off the edge of the page and into a completely different story by a writer he'd never heard of.

He was frightened by his peculiar plight!

"What if I don't fit in? What if the other characters hate me?" were his twin concerns as he glanced around.

He was in a residential suburb of a city. Above the modest roofs of the beehive houses, oddly shaped towers rose in the hazy distance; and a low rumble of traffic reached his ears like… He frowned, unable to think of a simile. Like chastisement, he eventually decided. Whilst congratulating himself on this comparison, a hand suddenly tapped his left shoulder and a voice rasped, "So you came at last!"

Thornton hadn't seen or heard anybody approach. And yet this was an enormous man to be so stealthy; his muscles bulged so conspicuously that they were more like geological features. He was bald, tanned and dressed only in long johns, apart from his massive feet, which were hirsute, pallid and scabbarded in transparent slippers. His veins throbbed and his cheeks glowed with relief. He leaned closer.

"Allow me to introduce myself. I am the Musulman Muscle Man. I am responsible for bringing you across."

Thornton shook his head firmly and replied, "That's incorrect, it was a simple accident. I went too fast and missed my turn and switched texts. It might happen to any fictional cyclist."

"Yes, but it was I who sabotaged your brakes!"

"Impossible. Only the author of my story could do that, and you aren't him, that's for sure. What's going on?"

"You misunderstand. I begged the author of your story to do it. And he obliged on a whim. Typical of him."

Thornton digested this news. It was plausible enough. So he narrowed his eyes and stared at this stranger in the way that characters used to stare at strangers in novels. Most don't bother now. "But why did you beg him to do that? Was it blatant mischief?"

"Heavens no! What do you take me for? I'm a moral fellow every day and normally wouldn't dream of abducting, directly or indirectly, anyone from a different fictional universe, but this is an emergency. I have a wife and I'm terrified of her. She's expecting me back home any moment but I can't face meeting her. I want you to go instead. Pretend to be me. Stroll into my house and say hello to her..."

"But I look nothing like you!"

"That's the point! My wife would suspect trickery if a man turned up who was a perfect replica of myself. If she sees someone who is the exact physical opposite of me, her suspicions won't be aroused. She'll assume that no deception is taking place."

"Your wife is a simple minded woman?"

"By no means!" The Musulman Muscle Man glowered at Thornton as if he resented this mild disparagement of a female he himself intended to brutally deceive. It's a common paradox, another case of 'I'm allowed to complain about it but you aren't'. Thornton had encountered this attitude often in his life. He sighed and said:

"Don't you have any friends or neighbours to ask?"

"Yes, but... they aren't human."

"Your request has unnerved me to a considerable degree. I don't like the fact my author colluded with you to put me in this position but there's nothing I can do about it on my own. My author never listens to me. Who knows why he favours you instead?"

"I'm the Musulman Muscle Man, that's why. I lift his spirits when he feels down, I'm really that strong."

Thornton capitulated. "I don't suppose I have any choice in the matter. If I do what you ask, will you guarantee that I'll be returned to my own story, the tale I'm meant to occupy?"

"I can't actually promise such an outcome, but I swear to intercede on your behalf with your author. And I'll look after your bicycle while you enter my house and greet my wife."

"Which house is yours?" Thornton squinted.

The Musulman Muscle Man pointed at a beehive that looked the same as all the others in the area. "There."

"But what shall I say to her when I go inside?"

"Just the usual. You know."

Thornton nodded. "Hi honey, I'm home!"

I used to have robes and a turban (wrote the Musulman Muscle Man) but as I grew stronger and stronger they burst apart. Then I knew I was ready to enter the Mr Universe competition.

But that event isn't just about physical force.

No, mental discipline is required too. And spiritual focus. I trekked to Yuckystan to find a guru to engage. To employ, I mean, not to marry! At last I found the Smarmy Swami. He coached me. He drove me in his old bus to his base. It was covered in flakes of burned wood and a male sheep wandered about on its own. "Ashram!"

The Smarmy Swami stopped the bus. I got out.

"This is my pad," he announced.

He wanted me to read between the lines.

But I didn't know how. That was one of the things I needed coaching for. Nonetheless, I settled in nicely.

My mystical education began immediately.

The Smarmy Swami taught me to meditate, contemplate, levitate and masticate. He taught me to gravitate. He taught me to gesticulate. But he never taught me to do anything rude.

I spent six months at the ashram and my mind expanded so much that I had to roll it up like a carpet every single night to get it back inside my head before I went to sleep. Luckily, some nights weren't single but had long-term lovers, and then it was acceptable to leave my mind expanded to its fullest extent, like a prehistoric sea.

Finally I was ready. I bade a farewell to the Smarmy Swami and paid his fare (well, I had to) on his bungalow stairwell. Like all bungalows it only had one floor, but that floor was vertical. Anyhow, I girded my loins and evaded the lions and set off anew.

The Mr Universe competition for the year Umpteen AD was due to be held in Grimwood City. I went there and registered my name. For a week I did battle on the stages of Body Hall.

My rivals were immensely forceful entities, half giant, half vegetable, half cliff, half badly added fraction, half recycled joke, and the ones with roots planted in the stage floor were certainly no pushovers. But I won at the end. Sheer determination on my part.

I stood on the podium and accepted the medal. A disc carved from the heart of a neutron star, it was. Dense.

Only Mr Universe is strong enough to wear it.

And then I hiked back here.

But on the way home, I started thinking about many things. About my domestic situation, about my wife and how terrible she is with that nest of venomous springs on her head. I told her not to get her snakes permed but she didn't listen. Hot tongs hissed and the serpents hissed back and I bet secrets were shared between them.

The fact I had married a gorgon was my own fault. I had prayed to my author for a 'gorgeous' bride and I guess he misheard. Or perhaps he just decided to play a mean joke on me…

I reached the outskirts of my suburb and I was trembling all over and my muscles were rubbing against each other like magnified walnuts, but then the author of the story adjacent to this one groaned loudly. The walls between the tales around here are so thin. Shoddy workmanship. I knew he wanted his spirits lifting again.

So I obliged. I lifted them as high as I could.

Much higher than ever before!

But I was still distracted by my predicament and my anxiety made me clumsy and to my horror I dropped them. I dropped his spirits! And they jarred as they hit the hard ground.

Something broke inside them. And the author hasn't been right since. He sprawled over into this text, even though it doesn't belong to him, and made changes. Random alterations.

I believe he's gone mad, frankly. And that explains why things happen in the new stories he writes that make no sense at all. And not only in his own work, but in the work of any author that he can reach from where he is. The houses in this suburb suddenly turned into beehives. That was the first change I noticed. Not the last.

You see those towers in the distance? They are gigantic flowers. And that low rumble you noticed isn't traffic but the hum of the occupants of the beehives. Yes, it's obvious now.

But as for my wife. Ah! Don't expect her to be a bee. She was always sweeter than that, so sweet indeed that she went over the ultimate edge of sweetness and returned at the bottom, where the sourness and bitterness is extreme, unbearable, even demonic.

And that's why I'm scared of her.

Listen. It's your bicycle that can travel between stories. That's what I asked your author to do. Invent a bicycle that can roll over the margins of texts and enter those written by other writers. You brought it here for me and now I plan to steal it. I'm sorry.

But at least I've left this letter in its place, to explain my actions. And if you survive the encounter with my wife, you'll be able to read it at your leisure. Good luck. And best regards!

The Musulman Muscle Man

Thornton pushed open the unlocked door. He found himself in a hall and at the end of the hall was another door and beyond this door he heard the sound of something creaking oddly.

He preferred orthodox creakings, Thornton did.

But he persisted with his quest.

He reached for the handle, turned it and yanked the second door wide. Before his eyes had time to register the scene beyond, he stepped bravely over the threshold. Then he blinked.

What he saw was remarkable but not evil.

A pyramid of honey jars that reached almost to the high ceiling. Many different kinds of honey were present here and some jars were positioned upside down; and of these, a few had leaked through their screwtop seals and slow cascades of honey poured down the glass sides of lower jars. It was an endless oozing, primeval and sickly. Runny honey and solid, clear and cloudy, crystalline and smooth.

And there was no doubt this was the wife.

Transformed into a ziggurat of the trapped congealment of bees' love. An unusual change for a woman!

Even more bizarre for a gorgon, surely?

Floorboards creaked under it.

And it was tall, tall, tall, this sticky structure.

Hundreds of jars, thousands.

So Thornton said the only appropriate thing:

"High honey! I'm home!"

The pyramid of honey jars seemed to sigh. Then it said sternly, "I can see that, but why pick a bungalow?"

"What do you mean?" gasped Thornton.

"You've turned into a home, just as you announced, but couldn't you have chosen to become a castle or a mansion or a manor or even just a big detached house with a garden?"

Thornton staggered to the nearest mirror on the wall. He had changed without any warning into an abode. A vertical bungalow. In the highest window of the house he saw a tiny face with a matted beard, a face that laughed before it squeaked words:

"I am the Smarmy Swami! Welcome to my ashram!"

Thornton blundered his way out.

The Musulman Muscle Man had scarpered.

Thornton picked up his note.

But he typically read the wrong side first.

P.S. Since I won the Mr Universe competition and became Mr Universe himself, I've noticed internal changes too. I'm cooling down. My cells are dying one by one, some turning into black dwarves, others into black holes. I've stopped expanding, no matter how much I eat. In fact I think it is likely I'll start contracting soon and probably I'll turn into a singularity that will explode and start the entire process again. A universe is like a set of lungs, breathing in, out, in, out.

And each breath is the lifespan of a single creation.

THE INFRINGEMENT

The door burst open. Three men rushed into the garret like a wedge of frozen spite. Thornton Excelsior dropped his brush in fright and turned to confront the intruders with wide eyes.

"There he is!" they shouted.

Two of the men were police officers. They stepped forward and seized him, dragging him away from his easel.

"W-w-what's going on?"

"You're a thief!" came the contemptuous reply.

"No, I'm not. I've never stolen anything in my life!" protested Thornton. "I just paint animals!"

"Exactly! I'm a photographer and I took the photo of that rabbit that you are painting. You're a plagiarist!"

"B-b-but..." stuttered Thornton.

"Copyright infringement," said one of the police officers.

"Come quietly," advised the other.

"I was just using the photograph as a guide. There's no harm in that, surely?" objected Thornton weakly as he gazed at the unfinished bunny on his canvas.

"A likely story!" The photographer drew a knife and lunged forward, slashing the picture to ribbons.

Later that night, the photographer sat at home, rubbing his hands together with malicious glee. His name was Jabberworth Sneek and he loved taking legal action against artists who 'borrowed' his images. He was an award-winning wildlife photographer and prints of his best images covered his walls.

Suddenly the door burst open. Three giant rabbits hopped into the lounge and one of them cried, "There he is!"

Two of the rabbits were dressed in police uniforms.

"What's the meaning of this?" blurted Jabberworth.

"Thief!" growled the first rabbit.

"No, I'm not. I've never stolen anything in my life!" protested the photographer. "In fact I go around prosecuting artists who break the copyright laws."

"Really? But I'm the rabbit that won you an award last month. You stole my image and never paid me for it!" And it nodded at one of the portraits framed on the wall.

"B-b-but…" stammered Jabberworth.

Before he could get his words out properly, the rabbit policemen bounded forward and gave him a thorough hopping.

THE TELEVISION

Technology allows the outside world to enter our homes in ways our ancestors would have found baffling. Unless those ancestors had been futurologists, Thornton Excelsior decided as he settled into his most comfortable chair. Like a domestic explorer trapped in upholstered quicksand he sank lower and lower until only his head and a single arm remained visible. But he didn't panic.

A luxurious seating arrangement was essential for what he planned next, namely the watching of his brand new 3D television. This was an expensive and sophisticated piece of equipment that dominated one end of the room like a cube of vacuum levered out of the dark of outer space. Thornton had the power to glow the inhuman void into life, to boil away the nothingness with the faintest plasma hiss.

His free hand clutched the remote control...

The jab of a button and the cube exploded with light, pushing moving images into the room. The effect was remarkable. As the images became stable and synchronised themselves properly with their roles, Thornton felt that he was standing among them, the characters of some historical drama, and that the room itself had changed, acquiring period furniture that overlapped or absorbed his own. He gasped.

Exulting in his illusory power, he switched channels, surfing the frequencies to find the show with the most awe-inspiring pictures. There was a fantasy about a cyclops and his understandable fear of unicorns but the acting was clunky and detracted from the marvels of the landscape, the crags and twisted trees that had invaded Thornton's house. So he lingered on it for only a few minutes before moving on.

A guru sat on a rug and dispensed his wisdom. "Just be yourself," he said. "If you are a fool, act like a fool. If you are an idiot, act like an idiot. If you are a buffoon, act like a buffoon. Don't pretend to be something you aren't. If you are a fake, be an authentic fake. Don't be a phoney fake." He smiled and winked his third eye.

Somewhere behind him, unseen, a triceratops brayed.

Thornton nodded vigorously. "I hate phoney fakes! I've known plenty in my time. You meet someone and instantly mark them down as a fake and then years later you discover that they really are heroic and did rescue a child from drowning and you realise you've been duped again! But I don't think wisdom helps much. Just look at the world!"

He switched channels. A crime thriller…

It wasn't a genre he had particular affection for, but he found himself quickly gripped by the plot of this show. A team of burglars were trying to break into a foreign embassy. They managed to force a window with a crowbar and climb into the building. They stood all around Thornton and played a torch beam over every available surface, including his forehead. They wore masks and dark unbranded clothing.

The show paused for a commercial break. The first advertisement featured robotic chimpanzees drinking cups of tea.

"I need a warming beverage too," Thornton said to himself. He decided to go into the kitchen and boil water in a kettle before the crime thriller came back on. But getting out of the chair was difficult. Fortunately the next advert was for rope ladders. He reached out with his free arm and grasped the lowest rung of one of the samples and pulled on it to extract himself from the deluxe trap. He came out with a massive slurp.

In his kitchen he moved as briskly as possible.

He rattled a spoon against a mug, urged the kettle to boil faster with this impatient tribal rhythm. He could hear the adverts capering in the other room. Then the water was sufficiently hot and he poured it over the teabag and stirred mercilessly. The adverts stopped, the commercial break was over. The thriller had resumed! He paused and listened to confirm this and he was rewarded with the furtive shufflings and whispers of the burglars.

In his slippers he ran along the corridor, the tea held out before him and emitting steam like the chimney of a locomotive.

Just before he reached the room the burglars stopped shuffling.

He entered to confront silence.

And also emptiness…

They had taken everything of value, including his most comfortable chair. All the ornaments on all the shelves were missing. The rug was gone, the antique clock on the wall too, the elegant lamp also! The villains had even stolen the 3D television, pulling

129

it back with them when they fled, drawing it into itself. Thornton stood numbly for many minutes. What sort of lowlife scum steals its own mode of entry and exit?

At long last he felt calm enough to sit on the floor and stare at a blank space while gulping his cold tea.

THE LOCK OF LOVE

The asteroid spelled disaster for the Earth. D-I-Z-A-S-T-A. Luckily, asteroids can't spell… Hands in his pockets, Thornton Excelsior walked down the street. His pockets were very big and crammed with hands.

He opened the gate of every house he passed, trudged up the gravel drive and posted a hand through the letterflap.

Sometimes dogs on the other side yapped. Sometimes cats yowled. Less often weasels, hippos and yetis guffawed. The asteroids bounced off the upper layer of the atmosphere, cricket balls on a dustbin lid.

There was a shout from an upper window: "Modesty Blaise!"

Thornton turned quickly, eager to set eyes on the enigmatic female adventurer, but she wasn't there. He had misheard. His humility was on fire. A bucket of water crashed down on him from above.

The flames were soon out… Out and about.

Dripping, he continued his task with dampened spirits but renewed physical vigour. He really knuckled down to it, Thornton did.

Before he could post the next hand, the door opened.

"What do you want?" creaked a voice.

"Thornton Excelsior at your service. I'm an arms dealer. Just slipping a promotional hand through your letterflap."

"At my service? At my service? But I'm not dead yet!"

"Congratulations! Who are you?"

"Formerly my name was Shylock. But I went on a course for merchants with low self-esteem and now I'm known as Brashlock. I still want my pound of flesh but modern regulations mean that I must be wicked in metric. Too bad, too bad. Do you have a fingerless glove for this promotional hand? If so, I'll take it and rub it. If not, then good riddance!"

Thornton discovered that many of his potential customers in this area were wrist-averse. He had dried out in the sun now. High

131

above, a pterodactyl flapped ponderously, blotting the landscape below with wing-shaped shadows. Asteroids cast their own shadows on the upper surface of the creature's wings. An enigmatic female adventurer ran down the street shooting a pistol.

She used a shotgun to shoot the pistol. But why?

A yeti sat on an inverted dustbin.

"Is this your house? Do you live here?" Thornton asked.

"I've been thrown out."

"May I interest you in a promotional hand?"

"No, I'm vegetarian."

"Would you like a job as my assistant?"

"What if you give me the elbow?"

It was a good question. Or maybe it wasn't. Working together, they were soon out of hands. Thornton and the yeti returned to the arms depot. Tonguewaggle Chipchop, the lawyer, was waiting in the office. "Now look here," said Tonguewaggle and they looked but saw nothing. "There have been complaints. The way you conduct your operations. People don't like free hands!"

"Would they prefer carte blanche?" Sarcasm from a yeti.

"They wouldn't, no they wouldn't. And even if they did, if they did, it wouldn't do them much good. Wouldn't. D'ye hear?"

"Goodness," said Thornton. His empty pockets flapped.

"If you want to fight me, if that's your attitude, then I'm willing to!" spat Tonguewaggle as he reached into his own pockets for cricket balls and began hurling them with immense force at his deadly enemies.

Who defended themselves with dustbin lids.

Let me tell you, gentle reader, what I invented this morning. A new kind of front door lock in the form of an ear. You just need to bend forward and whisper a secret word into it and the door will open on a spring. You can change the secret word as often as you like. I recommend the following word. Censored. Observe carefully as I program my own earlock. Now why did that happen? Why did a yeti's hand come through the letterflap and strike me on the tongue?

The publisher frowned and looked directly out of the page. "I can't publish this story as part of a linked collection, I'm sorry. It just doesn't fit in with the others. And in fact the others don't fit in with themselves. Thornton Excelsior himself isn't too keen on this one and he doesn't even exist. I think that says a lot about the state of your prose, really I do."

Brashlock has programmed his secure ear with the word 'flesh'. The yeti has programmed his dustbin with the word 'snow'. Modesty has programmed her enigma with the word 'gun'.

Thornton kissed his beautiful young lock. He used his tongue. Tonguewaggle Chipchop didn't emulate him. He had a reputation. He was sure he'd left it around here somewhere. Certain.

No sooner had I recovered from that blow on my tongue than the roof of my house collapsed on me. An asteroid had hit it. They had learned how to spell at last. I crawled painfully from the rubble. Rubble means trouble, let me tell you. Please won't you let me?

Thornton Excelsior happened to be passing. He was holding hands with his lock. "Help me!" I gargled on throat blood.

"Sorry, I'm in a hurry now," he snapped back.

"Where are you going?" I croaked.

"To see Reg I. Starr, the chief registrar of the Registry Office. We intend to get married, this darling ear and I."

"How is that feasible? How? How?" I wailed.

"Asked for my hand in marriage, it did. Hands, I should say. Plural. As easy as that, it was. And I had plenty spare. How could I refuse such a request? Romance may be buried but it's not quite dead."

SHEER LUNAR SEA

It was a very long time ago that the moon had authentic seas full of water but Thornton Excelsior recalls with vivid accuracy how he used to paddle across them in pursuit of his one true love.

He knew the Sea of Serenity like the back of his front, because there weren't hands back then. Not evolved yet.

No natural hands, that is. Artificial hands were everywhere. Thornton had tentacles, three of them, very flexible.

He was a typical moon-dweller, in other words.

A good idea, methinks, to look inside other words whenever you find any, because they must be packed with an implausible number of things. It appears that almost anything can fit inside those other words. Cut them open and watch the treasures spill out!

Thornton was tanned and youngish and intrepid.

The Casual Caress was the name of his vessel and he had bought it off Captain Dangleglum the previous year. Like all lunar ships of that time, it had a windmill bolted to the deck and the winds turned the arms and these rotated, in their turn, a pair of paddlewheels.

So it worked best when heading into the wind, which is the opposite of Earthly ships with their fussy sails and all that billowing and rigging, but it was many aeons before those came along.

The paddlewheels were carved in the shape of huge hands, so on every stroke they caressed the ocean but without an excess of passion, hence the name of the ship. Thornton employed two crewmen to help him maintain the workings of the cranks, cogs and levers.

The water churned beneath the creaking mechanism.

One of the crewmen was myself, the author of this story; and the other was you, the reader of it. That might seem odd now but it was normal all those millennia ago. The rules have changed.

These days, readers rarely take an active part in fictional tales. They're expected to meekly listen, not get involved.

Maybe there were fewer available characters back then and that's why authors and readers had to fill in? I don't expect you to remember any of this. It was millions of years ago, billions.

"Shift her up a gear, will you, Reader!" Thornton called suddenly. He was standing at the prow of the vessel with a spyglass raised to his central eye; and you pressed the clutch in response, wrestled with the gearstick, altered the ratios of concealed cogwheels.

The giant hands threshed the foam more fiercely.

"What have you seen?" I called.

Thornton was silent for a minute, then he lowered the spyglass with a sigh. "I'm not sure, just a speck on the horizon, but it could be her, it may be her ship! My quest might be over!"

This wasn't the first time he had got excited over a floating log or the stomach of a sleeping lunar sea otter.

And his heart beat more rapidly, pulsing on his sleeve like a pudding, because that's where we wore our hearts back then, just above the cuffs of our shirts, and most of our other internal organs were positioned on the outsides of our bodies, on our clothes.

It was our way. I won't say it was better than now.

I went into the galley to make a pot of proto-coffee for the three of us, while you, the reader, kept your strongest tentacle on the tiller of the ship, and Thornton climbed the spiral staircase inside the central deck windmill to the rickety balcony at the summit.

From up there, he had a better view of the speck.

"Is it her?" I called, as I came out with the tray of coffee mugs, purple steam curling from them like the ghostly tusks of a wild metaphor boar. I guessed the answer before he gave it:

"No, it's just a gigantic punctuation mark, a full stop. I thought I asked you to be more careful with your ink!"

"That's not one of mine!" I protested. "I have never visited this part of the text before. There must be another writer trying to collaborate on the tale without telling me first. I hate that." Then I decided to attempt to feel more charitable. "Maybe he got lost?"

"It's just a full stop without any words in front of it. I really don't like the look of that. Steer well clear! If we hit it, we might never get past it to the next sentence of our shared destiny."

Grumbling, with the spyglass tucked in one of his three armpits, poor old Thornton Excelsior descended and accepted a cup of coffee. He was so smitten that his bittersweet melancholy oozed off him in cubes, like a fussy geometrical sweat. Infatuation!

The woman he pursued was as elusive as the reflection of a shadow, a charming dream bubble, unpopped.

She was Molly Bergère, the Can't Can't dancer.

He had met her on the Rue of Regrets, that infamous street in which a plethora of sighs expelled by the passing people turns the sails of the red windmill that rears above the nightclub where the Can't Can't girls dance and caper on the curved gilded stage.

There and then he had decided to make her his!

And against all expectations, she had agreed to go away with him, the moment he entered her dressing room with a bunch of crystals on stalks, perhaps because of his charmingly awkward manner, his sincerity or his sense of fun, clear below the shyness.

But she had other suitors, Molly did, many others; and on the eve of her departure with Thornton, one of them decided to preempt him in the most precipitous way, by abducting her and fleeing to a land where they would never be found, across the ocean.

His name was Stanislaw Lemington Spa. He was a formidable rival, a clever fellow, and no one knew what he looked like. There was a rumour that he sloshed when he moved, but Thornton didn't find this information helpful when he resolved to get Molly back. He wandered the streets of every town on the moon looking for her.

Finally there was nowhere left to search but the open sea, so he bought the ship and set off. It was a desperate measure really, but what else could he do? Periodically he called for her through a megaphone from the deck and listened to the answer of the wavelets that broke against his hull. We both felt pity for him, the reader and me.

But what could we do to discourage him? Nothing.

And he paid our wages on time…

But to return to the main thrust of the narrative, let me remark that my theory about how another author, an unwanted collaborator, had entered this story surreptitiously received a boost when one of the fingers of one of the paddlehands was chewed off.

I rushed to the rail and peered over and saw—

"A mermalade!" I shouted.

"What's that? I never heard of such a thing!"

"It's like a mermaid but with thicker rind. Bigger teeth too. They don't exist, that's a fact, so the renegade writer, the one who is so careless with his punctuation marks, must have inserted it into this story. If we increase speed we might be able to outrun it!"

136

Thornton considered my advice. He puffed and smarted and the effect was quite odd, like a locomotive in a tuxedo; but even odder was the fact it was only 'quite' odd, rather than 'very' odd. And the oddity of having a pair of drastically different oddities in such close proximity was in itself a third kind of oddness. He nodded.

"Full handiwork ahead, dear Reader!"

And you changed gear again and we accelerated away. But it's never a simple task to beat a mermalade in a race and it caught up with us and bit off another finger from the same side and now we had fewer digits on the starboard wheel and our course veered.

"Keep her to port!" Thornton commanded.

You adjusted the tiller to compensate, but no sooner had you done this than the mermalade bit off yet another.

I realised that the attack was deliberate. Stanislaw Lemington Spa was the rogue writer! He was fighting back. But this suggested we were close to his hiding place, to Molly Bergère.

Whether Thornton had also come to this conclusion, I can't say. Back in those days we had no means of defending ourselves from monsters. No harpoons or grenades. A gentler age.

More crunching and swallowing and our ship turned in an even tighter curve, compelling you, the reader, to compensate even more dramatically with the tiller; but there was a strict limit to these precise adjustments, for when the rudder reached a certain angle it would stop, horizontal with the back of the hull, and *The Casual Caress* would become unsteerable, stuck in an endless circle, an eternal noose.

"Can't we bribe it to go away?" Thornton asked.

"I think not, I know not — by which I mean that I know for certain the answer is 'no' and not that I don't know — but maybe we can distract it by singing and dancing for its pleasure?"

Thornton's tentacles, all three of them, tugged his forked chins, both of them, as he analysed my recommendation. Finally he consented to the immediate production of an impromptu cabaret on the deck of the vessel so that the mermalade would cease biting the hands that fed it and gawp at our antics instead. Worth a big try!

I went first, reciting my latest story, the one you happen to be reading right now, this tale, but I got no further than the opening sentence of the second paragraph before I stopped. "He knew the

137

Sea of Serenity like the back of his— What's the problem? Oh, the mermalade isn't listening to me. It has chewed off another finger."

"And another," said the reader, wincing.

"And yet another," added Thornton. "Your recital is making no impact on it at all, Mr Author. I suggest that Reader here has a go." And he gave an encouraging nod in your direction.

You sang a comic song in full hearing of the mermalade, improvising rhymes so improbable that they guffawed at themselves, and projecting these verses with jocular resonance.

But the mermalade cared naught for your lyrical abilities. There was more crunching of wooden fingers.

So now it was Thornton Excelsior's turn. He tied his tentacles in knots and did a superb conjuring act, producing weepals from gleggs and durks from hankycheeks, and even though we had no idea what any of it meant we applauded until our suckers smarted.

But still the mermalade feasted on our paddles.

"We're doomed," I sighed.

And so it seemed we were. But then suddenly a vision appeared on the deck, a ghostly form of a female. I blinked, all six of my eyes, and so did you and so did poor old Thornton.

It was Molly Bergère, her spook in person!

She had expired from lovesickness and now her phantom had come to assist us in the extremity of our dilemma. She told us that she had been confined to the full stop we had spotted earlier, which acted as a floating island, until death had freed her.

She did a dance, a jig, in full view of the mermalade, kicking legs as high as she could, all nine of them, and undulating her long tentacles in the most sensual way imaginable.

The mermalade was captivated. It was mesmerised.

It stopped munching and froze.

She had petrified it with wonder, with amazement.

"Hurrah!" cried Thornton.

And we all cheered and threw our hats in the air, then we remembered that hats hadn't come into being yet, nor hatstands to go with them, and so our ardour was cooled somewhat.

It was further cooled by the fact that Molly had arrived too late to be of much use. The mermalade had chewed off every finger of every hand on the starboard paddlewheel. Not her fault: she was a ghost. But I think Thornton fell out of love that instant.

138

Molly Bergère faded away, back into nothingness.

"Let's get out of here before the mermalade recovers its senses and resumes chewing our ship to bits!"

That was my suggestion and it was a good one.

But without fingers on one side, we would simply sail in a circle for the rest of time. Then you, the reader, had an idea. If we plucked out the stiff feathers on our crests — did I fail to mention those? Too bad — we could attach them to the wheels in place of the missing fingers. So that's what we did and it worked well enough.

But there was an unexpected consequence of this.

The feathers tickled the sea and the sea began laughing and then we all realised that Stanislaw Lemington Spa didn't have a solid body like the rest of us, but was a sentient ocean.

That's how he was able to elude us for so long.

We were blithely sailing on him!

I don't recall what happened next, whether there was a fight or a truce was called, and neither does Thornton. But I bet you do. You: the reader. So the responsibility is yours, all of it.

That's what it was like when the moons had seas.

MY BEARABLE SMUGNESS

Thornton Excelsior was absolute ruler of the world only once and it was for a single season, but he accomplished much that was quite strange and even more that was downright bizarre.

He began his reign by systematically incarcerating everything that offended him. Enemies and rivals were thrown into dungeons. That's orthodox behaviour for tyrants; but Thornton went beyond the call of madness and took revenge on unexpected victims.

Cabbages offended his tastebuds. Put them in jail! Trombones offended his eardrums. Put them in jail too! Certain hairstyles, including his own? Dreadful and intolerable. Off to prison with them!

He once received an accidental blow on the head from a migrating boomerang and it gave him amnesia, but he locked his forgetfulness in an oubliette and recovered rapidly enough. Then he grinned.

"What do you think of my grin?" he asked his subjects.

"Unbearably smug!" they replied.

Thornton shook his head. "A brave answer but utterly wrong. My smugness can climb trees, fish for salmon with its paws and it loves the taste of honey. That makes it fully bear-able, I assure you. Now go back to the classrooms where you belong and revise yourselves adequately!"

His subjects were mathematics, geography and woodwork. They lumbered away on their abstract legs while Thornton adjusted his weight on the throne and rubbed his hands together in a dastardly manner.

"What shall I lock up next, I wonder?" he wondered.

He thought about it for some time and with greater insight than most despots might manage. "It has just occurred to me," he said, "that in fact I find jails offensive. So why don't I imprison them? Yes, that seems a reasonable thing to do. I'll put all jails in jail!"

And that was the order he gave. And it was carried out.

It wasn't carried out to the letter because all letters were already in jail, as were envelopes, stamps and postmen, but it was carried out in spite of that and also on a stretcher. The order had

140

fainted at its own audacity, you see. Buttons were undone on its bodice and it recovered.

Thornton played with his smugness in the meantime.

He preferred playing with it in the playroom but that was presently closed for renovation. The novation had failed.

A vast new prison was constructed to house all the jails.

In the meantime Thornton slept.

In the kindtime he awoke. His smugness had brought him breakfast. Honey on honey with a side dish of honey.

Thornton combed his hair as he ate. He had forgotten that his hairstyle was in jail. Sticky! Hexagons!

"I suppose I ought to visit my prisoners and gloat," he decided, "for that is what proper dictators do."

So he left his palace and skated with his smugness perched on his shoulder to the blasted region where the prisons were located. He roamed the dark corridors and peered into each cell as he passed. In one of the larger dungeons he saw a jail huddled in the corner and something inside him panged and he felt a wave of regret break into foam and bubbles within his heart.

"Poor little jail!" cried Thornton. "We must issue a reprieve and let it out. Where is the fat man with the big iron keys?"

"Don't you dare!" warned his smugness. "Have you forgotten that you recently made it illegal to change one's mind? If you pardon this jail you'll go to jail yourself! Who will pardon *you*?"

"But I make the rules!" objected Thornton.

"And I make sure you keep them! I'm stronger than you. My hug is grizzly in the extreme. Beware!" snarled his smugness.

Thornton kept his mouth shut. And when is a mouth not a mouth? When it's agape… No, wait a moment. Wrong joke!

They returned to the palace. But when night fell and the smugness was fast asleep, Thornton sneaked out and returned to the prison with a crowbar. "I'll have a martini," said the first crow. Thornton took the crowbar back to the tool room and selected a jemmy instead. And then—

"Shh! I've come to spring you from the clink!" he hissed in jail jargon. The prisoner woke up and blinked at him.

Thornton forced the door of the cell with the jemmy. The captive jail waddled over the threshold with difficulty. "What's wrong? Are you pregnant?" whispered Thornton. Then he realised that the jail contained prisoners of its own. In fact it was overcrowded. "Hurry up! Time is short!"

"No, I'm not," said Time, lashing a tail that was billions of years long, but it spoke offstage and Thornton didn't hear it.

The escape continued. But as Thornton and the jail were hurrying across the moonlit badlands, they came up against a wall of bars too thick and massive for the jemmy to bend. "What's this?"

"A logical development," answered the jail, "of your order to put all jails in jail. You see, the jail that was constructed to incarcerate jails also had to be put in jail, and that bigger jail also had to be put in jail, and so on, and so on, and so on. It's a life sentence!"

Thornton Excelsior is still a prisoner. How could he not be? His smugness tried to rule in his place but was overthrown by mathematics, geography and woodwork, who established a republic.

As for Thornton, there he is: mixing another cocktail at the late night bars of his cage and serving Time.

F   I   N   I   S

ND - #0512 - 270225 - C0 - 229/152/12 - PB - 9781907133879 - Matt Lamination